Sawbones
Memorial

Sawbones Memorial

Sinclair Ross

With an Introduction by Lorraine McMullen
General Editor: Malcolm Ross

New Canadian Library No. 145

McClelland and Stewart

ISBN 0-7710-9262-8

The Canadian Publishers
McClelland and Stewart Limited
25 Hollinger Road, Toronto

Printed and Bound in Canada

Introduction

After forty-five years in Upward, Saskatchewan, "Doc" Hunter is bidding farewell: "It's not the old days any longer. . . . The flu's over, the depression's over, the war's over. Big changes coming, just getting underway." Doc's words are not quite accurate; the old days are not really over. They remain to haunt the present and impinge upon the future. In *Sawbones Memorial* Sinclair Ross returns to the prairie setting of his earlier stories and novels, and through Doc Hunter and the townspeople of Upward takes us once more in memory through the pioneer days, the depression, and the prairie drought.

The setting is the patients' lounge of the new Hunter Memorial Hospital where townspeople have gathered to honour the departing doctor and to open officially the hospital named in his honour. The only piece of furniture of significance in this innocuous setting is the piano which had belonged to Doc Hunter's wife and which, like the old songs played on it, provides one of the leitmotifs of the novel and one of the links with past and future. Setting then is to all intents eliminated. Since the purposes of the gathering are to bid farewell to Doc and to open the hospital, the scene is designed for reminiscence and, at the same time, as talk turns to the new hospital and even more to the new doctor, it is a situation which looks to the future as well. The individuals gathered for a few hours in a single room, in a situation created for recollection and reminiscence, are all removed from their usual locale and activity. Time stands still as past and future come together in the present moment.

Sinclair Ross has indicated that it was from Claude Mauriac's novel *Dîner en Ville* that he conceived the idea of writing a novel through the words of a group gathered together for a few hours. As one of Mauriac's characters says, "While dinner lasts we are outside of time." Mauriac's individuals dine in a fashionable Paris apartment overlooking Notre Dame Cathedral, while Ross' characters munch sandwiches in a hospital lounge; yet the situations are similar. As in *Dîner en Ville*, in *Sawbones Memorial* there is no direct description, no introduction to characters, no narrative intervention, only the words of the various people who, for these few hours, are gathered here "outside of time." *Sawbones Memorial*, however, is more fluid than *Dîner en Ville*. Mauriac isolates six individuals in a static situation, seated around a dining room table; Ross' characters move about the room, chatting with one person or group and then with another, as conversational groups form, disperse, and re-form. Ross uses a cinematic technique, moving back and forth from group to group, pausing for snatches of conversation, close-ups, and occasional flashbacks in the form of interior monologues.

The first few pages set this process in motion. In a conversation between Doc and his old friend, Harry Hubbs, we learn that Doc is celebrating his birthday and his retirement on the forty-fifth anniversary of his arrival at Upward. We learn of his genuine concern for his patients and of his penchant for women. The main characters are mentioned: Dunc, Caroline, Nick, and Harry and Doc think back to "the old days," thus setting the reminiscent mood. Dialogue emerges like lines spoken in a movie or play, revealing personalities, giving essential information, and contributing to atmosphere.

The novel is composed of forty individual episodes varying in length from a few lines to twelve pages, and includes six interior monologues, two speeches, one dramatic monologue, snatches of conversation, and more extended conversations between two or more individuals. Although there is no psychological progression in the characters there is a gradual unfolding of the different personalities. The novel is carefully constructed so that our understanding of each person grows gradually as his name is mentioned from time to time in conversation or thought until, in many cases, we meet him in one of the conversational groups. Like Joyce's *Ulysses*, Ross' *Sawbones Memorial* is an expansive novel in which over thirty characters appear: the old and the young; farmer, teacher, housewife, and minister; the absent as well as the present; the dead as well as the living. Ross not only crowds his novel with characters but reveals beneath the surface a tumultuous Dostoevskian activity—including murder, suicide, incest, attempted rape, abortion, euthanasia—all aspects of the past of this seemingly ordinary little community which are unfolded gradually through dialogue and monologue. Each of the characters speaks in his own distinctive way. So involving is Ross' dialogue that we come to know those remembered as well as those present here and now. Thus Ida Robinson and Edith Hunter and Big Anna who are dead, and Maisie Bell and Nick Miller who are absent are as integral to the novel and as real to the reader as Doc Hunter, Harry Hubbs, Duncan and Caroline Gillespie. Pauses and interruptions are perfectly timed, scenes are carefully juxtaposed, monologues are interposed—all contributing to Ross' carefully contrived pattern. Seemingly inconsequential conversation renders personality and reveals underlying tensions, attitudes, preoccupations, and antagonisms.

Ross' handling of multiple points of view and different levels of discourse is probably the most outstanding technical accomplishment of the novel. He mingles interior monologue, dramatic monologue, dialogue, speeches, and songs. With no narrative outside of direct speech, speakers are identified by their manner of speaking and by the address of others. Interior monologues are identifiable by content, the seemingly casual inclusion of some remark early on that reveals the speaker; monologues are linked to dialogues by subject. In Mauriac's *Dîner en Ville*, two characters simultaneously and without any exterior dialogue recall the same incident. Ross uses a similar technique; one character converses about an episode from the past while another simultaneously reminisces about the same one. For example, Caroline Gillespie recalls her meeting with Nick Miller while visiting Dunc at a Canadian Army hospital in England. At the same time Dunc in an interior monologue recalls the same encounter. Such repetition of an incident from different viewpoints is analogous to the musical repetition of themes by different instruments.

Ross skilfully manipulates time to give us four generations of characters through the thoughts and memories of those present. Among the successfully realized characters are members of the early pioneering generation such as Ida Robinson, grandmother of Duncan Gillespie, Upward's leading citizen and chairman of the board of the new hospital. Ida is a determined and domineering woman. Like Grandmother MacLeod in Margaret Laurence's *Bird in the House* she remembers her superior Ontario upbringing and is not averse to reminding her family of it: "There had been a seven-roomed house with a red carpet and white lace curtains in the parlour, beautiful curtains. . . . There had also been a lawn with lilies and a pine tree. . . ." As is true of many of Ross' women, Ida dominates her weak husband. She finds some consolation and escape from the rigours of homesteading and a dull husband with young Doctor Hunter, also from Ontario. Another homesteader, but one who stands in contrast to the strong-willed Ida Robinson, is Harry Hubbs. Harry had left a small town in Nova Scotia for the west because of a series of incidents involving poker, other men's wives, and horse dealing: "I didn't exactly *have* to get out of town, but I wasn't helping things for my two sisters, both up in their twenties and starting to worry would anyone want to marry them. No future for me there anyway, so when the family raked up a thousand dollars – ." Through Harry's reminiscences Ross starkly describes the squalor from which Doc rescues him on the verge of physical and mental collapse from the loneliness and hardship of a life for which he has neither capacity nor will. After Doc has helped him settle into a job at the livery stable, Harry finds his true *métier* in the community, "branching out" as he expresses it, to making home brew, setting up poker games, and pimping for girls he brings from Regina.

The internal structure of the novel is cyclic. The time is spring, the date April 20 – the date Doc began his practice at Upward and now the date of his leaving it. As Doc retires, Nick is beginning; and he is returning to the town of his birth which he had left years earlier. The celebration itself, as a farewell to Doc and the official opening of Hunter Memorial Hospital, is an event which both looks to the past, to Doc's forty-five years here, and to the future, to the modern hospital and young doctor ushering in a new era. As Doc says in the concluding section of the novel, "It's all over and it's all beginning, there's nothing more required of you. April and the smell of April, just as it was all beginning that day too. . . . " Ross inextricably unites past and future: Nick is the new doctor; yet no one can think of him without thinking of the past as well; Hunter Memorial is the name of the new hospital, but its very name calls memory into play, calls up the past, the many years of Doc's practice here.

As do leitmotifs in music, words and phrases recur. Characters are linked by their references to others who are not there – Nick, Big Anna, Maisie, Edith. Objects call up certain individuals. For example, comment on the piano brings up the memory of Edith Hunter. Nick is defined by his thick boots and fur cap, which set him apart from the other boys who call him "Hunky," as his mother's black handkerchief and red socks both define her and set her apart from the other townspeople. Such repetition of words and phrases has a cumulative effect, recalling earlier incidents in which the same words or phrases were used, widening their implications, and ultimately operating as "objective correlatives," reverberating in the mind of the reader and awakening emotional responses. The recurrence of words and phrases, the repetition of names, the return to the same incident by different individuals – all contribute to the cyclic structure.

In another sense, the movement of the novel is centrifugal, beginning at the centre and circling outward, expanding to encompass the entire community, past, present, and future. The pivot is "Sawbones" Hunter who has been a participant in the lives of all the townspeople and yet, like most of Ross' central characters, has always remained to some extent an outsider. Thus, although ostensibly about Hunter himself, the novel is really concerned with universal human experience: love and sexuality, birth and death, youth and old age.

One major theme of the novel is communication and the failure of communication, the reaching out to another human being and the failure to reach out. As Doc says in his farewell speech:

– one of the things I'll remember, and will probably be puzzling over as long as I'm able to puzzle, is the damfool way you keep spoiling life for yourselves, bringing out the worst in one another. There's so much good here, and you keep throwing it away. . . .

A family doctor sees a lot of what's going on behind the scenes, and one of the things that has always impressed me is the enormous amount of sympathy and goodwill that springs up the moment someone is in trouble. When there's illness or death, the neighbours rush to help. No second thoughts – one question only: what can we do? They look after the children, bring food, wash clothes, sit up at night. I've often seen so much food coming into a house that the family has had to try giving some of it away again before it spoiled. But then the trouble passes, the household gets reorganized, and this little burst of spontaneous kindness, instead of helping to establish new relationships, make the town an easier, happier place to live in, sputters out in the old bitterness and spite. I'm not taking it on myself to lecture you. Your lives are yours, it's all behind me now, but I can't help saying what a pity, what a waste. . . .

Another main theme running through the novel, recurring in generation after generation, is that of the hypocrisy, pettiness, and prejudice of this small town. Ross reveals the unhappiness and at time ruinous effects of Upward's misconceived view of morality on the lives of many of the townspeople; on Nick Miller now returning as town doctor, on Benny Fox, the town musician, on Maisie Bell, the closest to a Scarlet Woman Upward has. One citizen remarks of Maisie, "The scarlet by this time must be faded to a pretty pale pink. Fifty-five if she's a day." Not faded enough, however; for although her parlour has been for many years Upward's only nursing home Maisie is not invited to the present celebration: "Ever notice how we've all got a good word for her, but we don't want to be seen in her company." So Maisie is snubbed while Harry, whose question-able activities, "favours for the city fathers," are more under-cover, is accepted. The disillusioned minister, a figure who re-calls Philip Bentley of *As For Me and My House* comments on the superficiality of the town's religious practice: "They sing *Praise God from Whom all blessings flow* with the assurance of the chosen, and there is not one word they understand. They bow their heads for the benediction, but their hearts are closed and dry." Despairingly he views his own role in Upward: "If I could only believe that despite it all I serve, that some day the seeds will spring and bloom, but I flutter on the margin of their lives like a leaf that has died and not yet fallen."

Sawbones Memorial is Ross' most innovative novel. By skilful use of time and associational memory he involves the reader in the hopes, fears, guilts, prejudices, and dreams of a cross-section of humanity. Upward becomes a microcosm of the world, through which it is shown that, although modern life has materially improved (Upward now has a modern hospital and the hardships of the homestead are long past), human nature remains the same. The name of the town is, therefore, ironic. In these few hours in the lives of Upward's townspeople, Ross explores universal aspects of the human condition, with skill and economy interweaving the tragic with the comic, and the sense of waste with the sense of hope, which underlie life in this and any community. Much of the tension of the novel evolves from the contrasting and counterpointing of the two polarities of man's experience: frustration and fulfilment, openness and hypocrisy, meanness and generosity. Ultimately, it is humanity itself with all its strengths and weaknesses which finds deepest expression in this novel.

Lorraine McMullen
University of Ottawa

"Ought to be ashamed, Doc, walking out on us at seventy-five. Just like a young fellow – good for another five years. What's Upward going to do?"

"Walking out, Harry, before I get kicked out. I read the signs."

"Some of the women, I suppose, wanting a young fellow for a change to fiddle around with them."

"Fiddling around's not exactly the way a medical examination is carried out, although I suppose it's true that some of them will feel safer with a younger man. Somebody a little more up-to-date."

"A lot of stories, Doc, that you used to have a pretty good way of fiddling round yourself. Horny old bastard, still shows all over you. I could name two—"

"Just two? I must be slipping. I thought I had a better reputation than that."

"Oh, you've got the reputation all right. In the old days, all the poor farmers' wives, a lot of them pretty lonely—"

"Well, in all modesty I think I can say I kept a few out of North Battleford asylum."

"Was that what you used to tell their husbands, that you did it just to keep them out of North Battleford?"

"Poor crops, long winters. I don't have to tell you what it was like. And their husbands with their own problems – a shave and a bath maybe once a week."

13

"Not all slicked up nice shirt and tie like Doc Hunter."

"At least not very attentive – a lot of work and worry—"

"Letting their wives get rusted up, eh? So that when Doc came along to take their pulse and things—"

"Most of the time, Harry, I was less concerned about the wife than about the farmer. Could he pay? How long would I have to wait? I had a lot of debts in the old days."

"I never paid you either for fixing up my boils – remember that day, the hell you gave me? – but you got it back a lot of times over, playing crooked poker. What's the town going to do, Doc? How many years did you say?"

"Forty-five. Forty-five today. My thirtieth birthday."

"You mean you landed here in Upward on your birthday?"

"That's right, April 20th, 1903."

"So that's why the opening's today! Nobody ever tells me anything."

"Dunc's idea – the official opening and a little farewell party together. Seventy-fifth birthday, sort of rounds things out. Forty-five years on call."

"It's not how old you are, it's how you feel. Look at me – I'm seventy-seven and I've still got all my teeth."

"That's right, Harry, seventy-seven and you're getting to be a bloody old bore. For the last ten years every time I see you you've been telling me you've still got all your teeth."

"More'n you've got, just the same."

"And I'm getting to be a bloody old bore too. I catch myself starting in again about 1918 and the flu – remember? – the trouble we had getting the graves dug fast enough. And the time I helped a woman with her triplets and then went out to the barn and helped the cow."

"The old days are worth talking about. Nick when he gets here, I'd like to see him take off his coat and help a cow."

"But it's not the old days any longer, Harry. The flu's over, the depression's over, the war's over. Big changes coming, just getting under way."

"Doesn't matter, you ought to hang on a while. Another five years anyway. It's your hospital by rights. You've spent your life working and waiting for it."

"By rights I oughtn't to have hung on this long. No place to go, nothing else to do – the war just gave me an excuse. A couple of days ago I had a boy with a sliver in his eye. Simple little thing like a sliver, and did I have a time! Couldn't see, couldn't hold my hand steady – the kid kicking and yelling and his father yelling back to hold still—"

"I had a sliver in my eye once and my Old Man just took a pair of pliers."

"And the last time Caroline brought the baby, it's got eczema, I saw her looking things over – not so immaculate as they ought to be, not so sterile. Mrs. Green's eyes are getting like mine – when she cleans she just hits the high spots."

"I've seen some English too whose things needed looking over. Remember Mrs. Pim? The one I used to get my bread from?"

"Yes, but you're not going to compare Caroline to Mrs. Pim. It's not easy, you know, coming a war-bride to a town like Upward with that accent and a lot of the women just lying in wait because she'd snapped up Dunc on them. A good girl, trying hard and keeping her head. But that day just the same it showed."

"In the old days before people worried so much about things being sterile we lived longer and were a lot happier too. Now it's all fads and fancy pills, and just look at the faces."

"Some of the fads are all right, and the pills too. I wouldn't mind being in Nick's shoes, thirty-three, just starting out."

"You could at least stay long enough to sort of help him get started. Why not? Introduce him round."

"New drugs, new ways of doing things – all over my head. Even when I try reading up on what's going on, half the time I don't understand. It's fifty years, you know, since I left Medical School. Always intending to go back – a year somewhere, to catch up – and things always getting in the way."

"Talking about new drugs, Doc, is it true there's one for blood poisoning? Just a needle and you're better straight away?"

"Almost straight away – a couple of days. I've used it a few times. It works. And I can remember when sometimes it would be nip and tuck for a couple of weeks, and maybe another month before you were back where you started."

"And is it true it cures the clap too?"

"That's what I read. Why, do you need it?"

"Not right now, but you never know."

"At first it seems you had to take it for a week in hospital, four or five times a day. Now they've improved it and one shot's enough. In the doctor's office – he's the only one who knows."

"Wouldn't it gripe you, though, coming up now with something like that and me seventy-seven. When I think back on all the times I didn't, just on account of being too scared."

"Talk about me being a horny old bastard! But right now I'd better move up front and start shaking hands. That's what I'm here for. It's my party, and I see Dunc's got his eye on me."

"How nice to see you looking so well, Doctor. We just want to add our congratulations."

"And many many happy returns. You must be very proud."

"Not much to be proud about, Mrs. Grimble. I've just been hanging on, sticking it out – same I suppose as most of us are doing."

"Well, whether you're proud or not we're all very grateful. You didn't have to spend your life in Upward. I'm sure you could have gone anywhere. Everybody is saying things will never be the same."

"And a lot of them are saying too it's about time. You don't remember Nick, he left eighteen years ago, but he'll do a far better job. A good boy. I used to take him with me on calls sometimes. I could see it coming even then."

"But it seems so unfair – all those terrible horse and buggy years and getting by with three or four beds in Mrs. Bell's parlour – and then when at long last the town builds a hospital it's not yours. Somebody else steps in and you move on. It's such a lovely little hospital – we've just been through."

"Well, it would be a bad day for Upward if I was the one stepping in. I've been looking it over too, touching things, half of them I don't even know what they're for. X-ray equipment, operating room. Dunc and the Board, you know, had to get advice from Regina. I couldn't tell them what a hospital this size ought to have."

"At least it has your name – *The Hunter Memorial*. I suppose you know there was a vote, town and country for twenty miles, The Upward and District Municipal Hospital or The Hunter Memorial, and you got it ten to one."

"That's what some of them call the cemetery too, The Hunter Memorial. I suppose I've done my share."

"Don't listen to him, Mr. Grimble, he's just fishing for compliments. He loves to have people tell him he's been our saviour. And I hope before he leaves you'll read him a lecture or two that he'll remember. In the last twenty years I'm sure he hasn't set foot inside the church half a dozen times. A fine example for our young people."

"Hello, Nellie, always popping up when you're neither wanted nor expected – a real newspaperwoman. But talking about compliments, I don't have to fish for them. That silly old bat of a husband of yours – have you seen how he's been writing me up for the paper?"

"Of course I've seen it. I wrote most of it."

"Brought it round and showed it to me this morning. Didn't know where to look – all set and ready for the front page Thursday."

"Dan, I said, it's a scoop. We don't have a chance to get rid of our old Sawbones every day so let's give it everything. Hip hip hooray! I dressed it up for him – the woman's touch. I was the one who put in the bit about the babies."

"Over a thousand, it says. A *thousand*, Nellie – have you gone crazy? That's more than twice the population of Upward."

"Well, if you sat down with your books and counted them up – forty-five years – you'd likely find there were a lot more."

"You know, Doctor, I wouldn't be surprised if Mrs. Furby's right. Forty-five years – it must be a record."

"Of course I'm right. You're going to read it Thursday in the *Chronicle* and what you read in the *Chronicle* is always right.

Forty-five years into one thousand babies makes just twenty-two babies a year, say a toe and a diaper over. And twelve into twenty-two makes not quite two a month. Now as long as I've known you, Doc, and that's at least twenty-seven years, you've always been rushing off with your little black bag to help some yowling unfortunate get his first good lungful of our Saskatchewan dust- and mortgage-laden air, so less than two a month is probably on the low side. Rose and I worked it out a few days ago. Isn't that right, Rose? Where are you?"

"I would say a very conservative estimate. A sparsely populated territory but throbbing with such enormous stores of reproductive energy. Oh, excuse me Mrs. Grimble – trust me to put my big foot in it – but you know what our Saskatchewan winters are like, our long Saskatchewan nights."

"How are you, Rose? You haven't been around to see me for a few weeks. Saving up all those imaginary ailments for the new man?"

"Maybe the new man will be intelligent enough to know they're not imaginary and prescribe something a little more effective than fifteen glasses of water a day to keep my kidneys flushed."

"Never mind, Rose, there's nothing like a well-flushed kidney to help you through a Saskatchewan winter. Isn't that right, Mrs. Grimble? But on the subject of reproductive energy, I don't suppose the thousand begins to tell the story at that. Isn't it true that in the early days having a baby was just something for the neighbours? Wasn't there usually a woman with a knack?"

"That's right, I was mostly for the complications."

"Breech deliveries, I suppose—"

"And a lot of times it was all over when I got there anyway. The phones didn't go everywhere, not in the early days, so someone would have to come or send word."

"And then, I suppose, they wouldn't want to pay?"

"Well, first things first. I've even had them turn on me, nice easy life, collar and tie, never dirtying my hands—"

"It would seem then, that that silly old bat of a husband of mine wasn't exaggerating after all."

"I'll tell you something Nellie, that you slipped up on: the horses."

"Yes, I know, and I'm sorry. It's just that so far as I'm concerned horses are not good copy. They trot, they gallop, they eat oats and at times they undoubtedly look very noble, but frankly I'm a man's woman."

"They were the ones just the same that got me there, the ones that took the beating. You've maybe heard me talk about a bay called Rip. I always kept two, so they could take turns, and then in winter when the roads were heavy I could use them as a team – but he was such a good horse, fast, willing, I didn't always play fair. Always pretending not to mind. Nice little whinny, wanting to rub noses—"

"If I remember right, Rip was the one that developed pneumonia? You whipped him up and left him standing in the rain?"

"He was the one. This day a boy came riding in nearly crazy, he'd shot his father. Here – in the thigh – blood coming in spurts —"

"October, right? They'd been shooting ducks?"

"Yes Nellie, *ducks*. I'm telling the story to Mr. and Mrs. Grimble. His own horse was in such a lather we turned it loose to go home itself and he got in the buggy with me. Only seven or eight miles but there'd been a rain and the roads were heavy. All mud roads in those days. Sometimes weeks on end there'd be spots you'd sink in up to the axles. Anyway by the time we got there Rip was in a lather too."

"And the boy just left him standing – neglected to put him in the stable and give him a blanket – right?"

"So scared thinking about his father, I suppose, he didn't hear me. And it was starting to rain again – heated up and then the chill. They were all good horses but he was the best."

"And the man, Doctor, the boy's father?"

"Pulled him through – one of those things. He ought to have been dead before I got there, the hole in his leg and the blood he'd been losing, but he managed to hang on. Husky and big. In those days people were better at hanging on. His wife didn't know about making a tourniquet but she'd wrapped a pillow round his leg and tied it tight. Cost me Rip, though, and I used the whip."

"In those days, Doctor, just how big was your territory?"

"Big enough. Suppose a hundred or so square miles."

"You don't multiply, Doc, any better than you divide. There wasn't another doctor, any direction, for twenty miles – and twenty miles by twenty miles is four hundred square miles. And that's very conservative too. The closest doctor was in Comet, twenty miles, but west and north it was more like fifty."

"They must have been such long drives, Doctor – sometimes, I suppose, three and four hours. What on earth did you think about?"

"Used to get caught up on my sleep, especially on the way back. I'd just leave it to the horse. A few times he put me in the ditch but not often. And sometimes I'd sing, nobody to hear me so no harm done. And recite poetry, see how much I could remember."

"Occasionally a hymn and a prayer, I hope."

"Well, yes and no – women having their babies when the weather was bad, or all coming together – I didn't always feel like singing hymns."

"Sorry to interrupt, Doctor. Let me fill your glass."

"Fill it, Caroline, and for Heaven's sake spike it. What's this stuff supposed to be, punch? Ten gallons of orange and cranberry juice and six ounces of gin?"

"Sh – not so loud. It's supposed to be *pure* orange and cranberry juice. Duncan's got some good Scotch for you but you'll have to wait. Remember they're going to take your picture and we want you standing up straight, looking respectable. And that's not till half-past ten."

"He's slipping, Nellie. At least every other time I see him now he tells the story about Rip and the man with the blood spurting from his leg."

"If it isn't Rip it's the flu epidemic – always the old days. You heard me try to head him off."

"He took Rip to heart a lot more than he did poor Edith. I can still see him at the funeral, not even a black tie."

"Dan, I remember, was furious. We wanted something for the paper, a few details about her family, and the prodding it took to make him hunt up a picture!"

"Although I suppose he had his problems. A strange woman – thought herself better than the rest of us, better than him too, likely. And absolutely no sense of humour."

"He might have tried, though, to spare her feelings, since appearances were so important to her."

"All the years I knew her, Ladies' Aid, the choir, working with her at church suppers – and give her her due she did work – I don't think I ever once heard her laugh. Not what you'd call a real one, all the way up."

"When you think, though, that she knew, and knew everybody else knew too – always hanging over her, the humiliation—"

"She could forget long enough to buy clothes and rig herself out in them. Remember the new outfits, spring and fall? The beaver coat, and then the Persian lamb? I suppose it was one way to get even."

"For all that, though, she took it hard. I'll never forget the time, years and years ago, when we were all standing on the church steps after service, six or seven of us, and Maisie Bell came along. The way she picked up speed when she saw us and put her head down. After all, we were the Good Women of the town, the Holier-Than-Thou's, God forgive us, and I suppose she had a pretty good idea of what we were thinking even if we weren't saying it."

"Old Mrs. Purdy – I wasn't there but I've often heard you tell it."

"That's right, with the squeally voice. She saw Maisie sprinting along but she didn't notice poor Edith standing right beside her. I'll never forget the nasty little laugh – 'Oh dear, she must be on her way to see the Doctor, maybe he's going to give her an injection.'"

"Now, Nellie, you're letting your reporter's imagination run away with you. I've heard you tell it many many times and there's never been a word before about an injection, just that she said the Doctor must be waiting, and then started to sing *I need Thee, Oh I need Thee, Every hour I need Thee.*"

"Anyway, poor Edith heard. I can still see her walking down the steps ahead of us, chin up, stiff as a ramrod, and the silence. She had a new spring hat with a yellow rose – the way it gave a little bob on every step—"

"A very handsome woman – trust Doc – and at least she knew how to wear the clothes. The nose on her – as if someone had trimmed it with a knife and ruler, just like a nose ought to be. Only so cold – you've often said it yourself. Such lovely hair, and such a lot of it, but the way she used to draw it back. I used to look at it and think if it was only mine."

"And he, I suppose, thought it was all just maidenly modesty – in those days there was such a thing – and that when he got his hands, etc., on her there'd be a great awakening."

"Exactly, her Prince Charming, and they'd live happily ever after. As a lady's man he never underestimated himself."

"Even the piano – *Star of the Sea* and *Rock of Ages with Variations* – I don't pretend to know anything about music but it always seemed to me she hit so *hard*. Playing the hymn at Ladies' Aid – I can still see her, sitting up so stiff and straight, making damned sure the Lord heard and sat up too."

"And *Redwing*, remember? *There once was an Indian maid, A shy little maid of old—*"

"Indeed I do remember. His birthday – funny you mention it, here it's his birthday again today – and her turn to entertain the Ladies' Aid. The way she had the music set out on the piano so we'd be sure to see it. Somebody made a remark – after all it did

22 .

seem a bit frivolous for Edith – and she said she'd just got it for the Doctor because it was his favourite, he was always whistling it."

"I remember – trying to sound so nonchalant, as if that was the way they lived, sharing things – a song like *Redwing* for his birthday—"

"I suppose it was a case of what the books call frigid. If ever there was talk about a girl being in the family way or anything like that she wouldn't just look shocked and all ears like the rest of us, she'd curl her lip as if it was something out and out disgusting, really dirty."

"Her mother, I suppose. They used to be like that."

"Although mine was bad enough. When you were taking a bath you weren't even supposed to look – and a lot of effect it had on me."

"Oh yes, Nellie, we all know what a high-stepping adventuress and wanton you are – Scarlet Woman of the Plains – and if a man was so much as to faintly leer at you you'd tuck up your skirts and run so fast—"

"Bring on your leer and try me. Dan's either slowing up the last few years or putting an awful lot of energy into the paper. But I won't dispute the Scarlet Woman title with poor Maisie. She's probably the closest to one we'll ever have in Upward. Do you suppose she'll be here tonight?"

"No, but she should be. This should be her party too. While we were waiting for the hospital, she filled in. A lot of times her parlour saved the day."

"Clean beds, good ham sandwiches—"

"When I was with her after George died she used to toast the sandwiches for me. Trying to be kind – she was sorry and didn't know what else to do."

"Ever notice how we've all got a good word for her, but we don't want to be seen in her company. As if it was going to rub off—"

"I know – people look the other way on the street, and then come running to be taken in. Johnny's broken his leg, or Mother's dirtying the sheets again and I've got to have a couple of weeks' rest."

"We ought to write her up for the *Chronicle* too – *Serving the Community for Thirty-five Years*. Now would be the right time when the hospital's opening and there's going to be no more need of her parlour."

"But you won't. You and Dan'll talk it over and decide maybe it's just as well to let things rest."

"We'll see. The scarlet by this time must be faded to a pretty pale pink. Fifty-five if she's a day."

"Do you think, Nellie, there was really much between her and Doc?"

"Well, there were always plenty of stories about Doc and the little extra services he gave some of his patients, and I suppose with so much smoke there was a little fire. I can believe it. Even yet he's got a roving eye. Didn't you notice him just now taking in everything Caroline's got to offer, up and down and over and under?"

"And Maisie does bounce very nicely, even yet."

"Provocative, I think, is what you'd call her walk. It's such a marvellous word and we never but absolutely never have a chance to use it in the *Chronicle*. Well, he was in her place a lot to see his patients, telling her what to do, when not to serve ham sandwiches, so it's only reasonable to suppose that from time to time they would turn to each other for relaxation and relief. At least he would turn to her."

"But not an affair – you know what I mean – losing his head —"

"Good Heavens no, not Doc. She was there, that was all – with the necessary. He's the sort that if he wasn't in the mood he'd look straight through her, walk off without so much as a good-night. And if he was in the mood – well, he was the Doctor."

"He probably thought he was doing the right thing – a sort of loyalty – but in fact he made it so hard for her. Stopping to talk to her in the street, having coffee together in Charlie Wong's, sitting close to the window to make sure everybody would see – deliberately giving people something to talk about."

"His way of showing what he thought of us and our self-righteous little world. And I suppose we had it coming."

"Only he never stopped to think that taking a stand made the town take one too – against her, not him. Trust the man to get off scot free – it never fails. I don't suppose many of us really cared if they had a few times together. If they'd just been a little more discreet, kept the blinds down, respectability would have looked the other way."

"And in the long run, poor Maisie was the one who paid."

"He didn't care about the gossip, so why should she? Her champion."

"Although give him his due it wasn't only Maisie. He was always on the side of the underdog, the down-and-outer. Look at old Harry what's-his-name over there, drooling into his glass as if somebody had just told him he's going to be strung up for his sins at dawn – bum, card shark, never did a day's honest work in his life – but Doc's always stuck up for him."

"I know. I don't suppose it's true but I've heard he even used to bring in girls from Regina and keep them for a week at a time down by the elevators in a boxcar. Five dollars for fifteen minutes, and he took half."

"Of course it's true – and poker games – but Doc's always had time to talk, always giving him a lift in his car. Cronies."

"And of course there was Nick. What is it he calls himself now?"

"Nick Miller – his own name, just short of a few Ukrainian z's and s's. Dan's only mentioning him this week as the new man taking over, but next week he's giving him a spread, a sort of *Welcome Home*. I suppose we'll have to get used to calling him Dr. Miller."

"I don't remember him very well – everybody just used to say the hunky boy – but I can still see his mother with the black handkerchief round her head and the red socks."

"Anna – Big Anna."

"You must sit down, Doctor, you're going to be terribly tired. Over here on this sofa, with me. There's something I want to tell you."

"Nobody I'd like better to sit down on the sofa with – prettiest woman in town."

"I hear stories that you're an old rascal and sometimes I think maybe they're true; but this is very serious and you mustn't laugh."

"I know, you want to run out on Dunc and come to live with me in Saskatoon. Well, I'm willing to give it a try – six months."

"No, I'm not leaving Upward with you – at least not right now – but I want you to know it was on account of you, partly on account of you, that I came."

"Dunc must have had a picture with him – an old one, before I started losing my hair."

"No, nothing to do with hair. How shall I explain? Surrey, you see, is such a long way from Saskatchewan—"

"I saw the snaps of course that Dunc sent his mother. You in the garden with the dogs, you and the roses, Dunc and you together with the dogs and the roses – your parents – it must have taken courage."

"My parents thought he was wonderful. Mother, I think, was head over heels in love with him herself, and Father's summing up was, not a pretentious bone in his body. But of course they weren't exactly happy at the thought of their only daughter setting out for the great Canadian Unknown. My friends all thought I was mad, and I myself wasn't quite sure."

"Well, I don't mind telling you, when I heard the girl in the rose garden was coming the first thought that went through my mind was she's either very brave or just another damfool limey."

"I used to lie awake trying to imagine what it would be like, asking myself could I ever possibly fit in. Everybody said wait and see. You're romanticizing him – he's a big handsome rawboned soldier come thousands of miles to fight for freedom and democracy – it sounds so wonderful – but what will you think of him when he's out of uniform and back behind the counter in his little country store?

"Well, as you know, he was wounded in France and they flew him back to a Canadian hospital, just outside London. I was working in London, and of course as soon as I heard I asked for an afternoon off and went to see him. Tears, embraces – my hero – but he had something else on his mind that day and it wasn't long before he showed me a letter he'd just received from his mother telling him Grandmother Robinson had died."

"Yes, Ida meant a lot to Dunc. And to me. In fact I was there when she died. She sent everybody else away, even Sarah for a few minutes, so we could have a last little talk."

"Well, after I had read the letter he lay back and began telling stories. The pioneer days – the things she had done just to survive. The little one-room sod shack, grass and weeds growing out of the roof – nothing to burn but dried dung. Buffalo chips, except that they weren't buffalo. The first winter, I think for three months, they had nothing to eat but boiled wheat and milk – an egg on Sundays and a chicken at Christmas. And then the time her husband had pneumonia and she had to ride four miles through a blizzard for a neighbour to stay with him and keep the fire on – Sarah was only nine or ten and she was afraid to leave them alone – and then on another twelve miles for you. But most of the way she had to get off and lead the horse so that her legs and feet wouldn't freeze.

"Grandmothers and blizzards were the last thing I wanted to talk about that day, you can understand. I wanted to talk about him, what it had been like, was he going to be all right, had they got everything out. He still had a bandage round his head and he looked so wonderful, just like a hero should look – and I kept interrupting him with my questions, trying to remind him of the living, while he kept going back to what that day seemed just the dead.

"And then, as if Grandmother Robinson wasn't enough, he started in with more stories about someone called Doc Hunter.

More early days – the red cutter and the buggy with the yellow wheels and the spanking blacks and bays. The storms he'd battled and the sleep he'd lost and the lives he'd saved . . .

"Then he broke off and I could see he was going on with it in his own mind. He had wanted so much himself to be a doctor – and then he broke that off too and came back to say he wished I could know you. He's so shy sometimes. It was his way of asking me again.

"I was impatient and yet I was taking it all in. You and Grandmother Robinson – the stories began to haunt me, until suddenly one day it was clear, and I said to myself that's what I want too.

"You see, I had always lived a rather useless life. My parents, my brother Eric – we were all useless. Not a great deal of money, but fortunate. We went to good schools, we travelled, we had that beautiful old house. Somewhere along the way, though, I had picked up a social conscience. Oh, not a very big or bold one: I didn't try running away to join groups and carry placards, nothing like that; but at least I knew I was having it too easy.

"During the war, you know, everyone young and physically able had to do something – a job or the Services, no exceptions. I wanted to join the Land Army – they plowed and grew things, looked after chickens and cows – but Father was afraid the work would be too hard and the other girls too rough. He wrote to someone and as a result, not protesting very vigorously, I'm afraid, I went to London for a typist's course and then to a job in Army Headquarters. Now do you see where you and Ida Robinson come in? You say I must have had courage but on the contrary I was afraid – of both Saskatchewan and myself. Terribly afraid. Would I ever be able to adjust to things? Would it be fair to Duncan to say yes and then fail? And at the same time I wanted so much to be part of it. A big new country, a country of beginnings. I wanted so much to be a pioneer too and do my share."

"And now that you're here?"

"It's all right because Duncan's all right. As to the brave new world I was looking for, the country of beginnings, of pioneers – well, last week it was my turn to invite the Ladies' Aid for their weekly meeting, and at four o'clock in the afternoon I served creamed chicken, hot biscuits, ice cream and frozen strawberries – oh yes, and chocolate cake – to about twenty-five women, most of them overweight, all in the name of and to the glory of the Lord."

"Upward, in other words, is imposing its will."

"A few days before, there had been a little explosion with Duncan's mother. It was my first time to play hostess on such a grand scale and she dropped over to see what she could do to help. I said bread and butter and a cup of tea is all they need – defiant, daring her to say they needed more – and for answer she just waggled a finger at Robbie in his carriage, you know how grandmothers do it, and after a little silence said very quietly, 'You've got to sell a lot of soap and tea, you know, to send a boy to college.'

"Duncan didn't make it; he had the store and his mother and brother; and like all good fathers he now has plans and dreams for Robbie. To do what he couldn't do – and so I understand my role."

"I wish you could have known Ida. I wish you could have told her what you've just told me. You'd have liked her. And I think she'd have liked you too."

"She'd probably have thought me terribly spoiled. My lovely little house with its hardwood floors and all the wonderful electric things in the kitchen. It's hard for me even to imagine a sod shack, dandelions on the roof."

"For that matter, Ida didn't live in the sod shack very long. Maybe two years, three at the most, and then they built a fairly good frame house. And I have my doubts about the buffalo chips. At times, maybe, to help out a bit and save the coal, but Ida's experiences never lost anything in the telling. The story about riding in for me when Nat had pneumonia, and leading the horse, is absolutely true. But three months with nothing to eat but boiled wheat and an egg on Sundays – well, with a bit of give and take it might have been true for three weeks – although myself I'd say three days, maybe after a bad storm and the roads were blocked. It sounds more like something she would tell Dunc when he came to visit her and was turning up his nose at the rice pudding or prunes. At that, you know, boiled wheat with a little milk and sugar isn't bad. I've tried it – better than oatmeal porridge any day."

"Now that's enough, Dr. Hunter, I'll have you know I married into a family of pioneers and unsung heroes, and that's where I'm going to stay married."

"Nothing to worry about, I couldn't spoil Ida on you if I tried. A lot of the women had it just as hard, some of them far harder, but she stood out because she had standards, her own laws. She didn't just survive, she came through with her head up, telling a joke on herself, ready for more. When she had to, busy times when Nat was out in the field twelve and fourteen hours a day, she'd put on a pair of old overalls and a smock and go out slopping round the stable, feeding pigs, milking cows – I've seen her – but she never slopped inside. Always dressed. It might be an old dress, patched and faded, but it was always clean and it always hung like a dress should hang. And she was always clean herself, always had her hair combed. You're looking at me and wondering what kind of woman wouldn't wash herself and comb her hair. Well, there were plenty. After a while they'd give up, lose heart. The poverty would get them, the isolation. The babies would come and they wouldn't keep them clean either. I've been to places, on calls, where even the floor was filthy – you never knew what you were stepping in. The mother with her hair in her eyes, the youngsters half-naked, maybe if it was cold with an old blanket round them, watching out of a corner like scared little animals. In summer, the flies—

"When I think about it now what surprises me is how most of them came through. Some of course were better stuff and never got that bad in the first place, but on a long trip I always took care to have cheese and crackers with me. That tells you something. They'd ask me to sit in with them for a meal and I'd say my stomach was cutting up.

"Ida, though, scrubbed and swept and was a demon after flies. I guess after poor Nat too. He was a good fellow but a bit slack. I was always glad of the chance to have a meal with them. Sometimes I'd even go a few miles out of my way. Always a good meal – she had a knack. Even when it was only homesteaders' fare, salt pork and potatoes. And it was a chance to slip a dollar under the plate. Big money, cash. They had their butter and eggs

– in summer it was usually all they had – but they had to trade them at the store for groceries. Sometimes for months, waiting for the crop to come in, they wouldn't have five cents.

"But that gives the wrong impression because it wasn't just to help them that I went. I liked going, enjoyed the meal. She talked a lot and it was good talk. She could always see the funny side – always had a new one about the neighbours. She'd come from down east, a little town near Owen Sound – White Picket Fence class – and she'd brought things. There was always a cloth on the table and a butter knife for the butter. You didn't dip with your own at her table.

"What's White Picket Fence class? Well, that's what I'd been myself – Ontario small town. My wife too, she'd come west to teach. The people on the right side of the tracks – ever heard that one? The lawyer and the doctor and the vet, some of the store-keepers and the Presbyterian minister – the Baptists and the Methodists and the Holy Rollers didn't always make it. Vegetable garden and potato patch at the back, out of sight, along with the clothesline and woodshed and doghouse, sometimes the stable; and a nice lawn with flowerbeds and sweet peas in front. Maybe some lilacs and elms, and of course a white picket fence. Get the picture?"

"By the sound of it you must have been terrible snobs."

"In fact, that's what some of the neighbours used to call Ida. After the first two or three years she had flowerbeds too, and a caragana hedge. Even a few Manitoba maples, and heaven help the hen or pig that crossed the line."

"So I did all right. It's a good family I married into even if they didn't eat boiled wheat and burn buffalo chips."

"One of the best. Sarah's one of the best too. Funny how families repeat themselves. The man she married was another slack one, Herb. Friendly, big-hearted – everybody had a good word for him – but there was a soft streak, he liked the easy life. Stan takes after him, Dunc after Sarah. You've got nothing to worry about."

"No one, it seems, ever has a good word for Stanley, but perhaps he's not altogether to blame. At least Duncan always defends him. He has that leg."

"And makes the most of it. Compared with what a lot of people have to go through life with, it isn't very bad. The year he was three or four we had a little epidemic of infantile paralysis, half a dozen cases – I suppose Dunc's told you – and he got off easy. Never needed crutches or a brace, just a little limp that you can hardly notice. Except when he's tired or wants you to feel sorry for him. Dunc went off to the war and got a medal while he had to stay home and look after the store. Breaks your heart the way he tells it. But the truth is he's just plain no-good. When Dunc was away it was Sarah who had to look after the store. Ten o'clock for him was early, and every so often he'd drive out to the farm to see how the cattle were doing and stay away two or three days. Just an excuse – he'd take a bottle and he and the fellow they've got out there working for them, Charlie something, they'd tie one on."

"Duncan worries. He wishes he wouldn't sing with Benny's band."

"And he shouldn't sing with Benny's band for the simple reason that he can't sing. It's terrible, and everybody knows about Benny. Benny's all right, twice the man some who make fun of him are, but a town this size, sooner or later there are bound to be some raised eyebrows."

"It's not so much the eyebrows that bother Duncan, it's Stanley himself. He just glories in it – *Don't Fence Me In,* and *Jealousy.*"

"That's it – he's anything but an asset to the band, so why does Benny let him?"

"Duncan of course never comes out and says that – in fact he has a soft spot for Benny – but I can see what's on his mind. . . . There, he's sending signals to me now. They're waiting and I'm taking too much of your time. But don't get up. You can hold court every bit as well sitting right where you are."

"You've been a real friend, Doc, and we just want you to know."

"We can't wait and that's why we're butting in like this but I said to George after all he's done we simply got to go. It's the very least, we got to say good-bye. Billy and everything, that's what I said to George."

"It's a cow. She's made small and it looks like she's coming in tonight for sure. That's why we got to rush – nearly lost her last time and I want to be around."

"And you know cows – just like her to start the minute our backs are turned but I said to George it doesn't matter we simply got to go and say good-bye. And take Billy, so he'll remember."

"Yep, this is Billy, Billy the Boss. Pretty well runs things. Since it looks like we can't have any more we're taking good care of him. Six in June – going to get a pony for his birthday, if he's good. Got a calf already and his own hens – making a real farmer out of him."

"Billy, this is Dr. Hunter. Now don't stand there with that look on your face, I want you to shake hands. Come on now, nothing to be scared of – shake hands."

"Makes shy sometimes, and then when he gets started you can't shut him up."

"Billy, you hear me! Shake hands! If it wasn't for Dr. Hunter you maybe wouldn't even *be* here."

"Come on, Billy, you want that pony, don't you?"

"Now I'm warning you – for the last time, shake *hands*!"

"That's the way. Wasn't so bad now, was it? And leave your coat alone, we're not going to stay."

"Sorry to be rushing off but that's the farm for you every time. Just like her to be into it right now."

"What you want to do, Doc, is take a nice long rest. Don't worry about anything, and keep well."

"If ever you're back this way be sure to come out and have a meal."

"That's right – now you be sure."

"And have a nice time in Saskatoon."

"You just do that now, be sure—"

"No, Mrs. Clarke, where we are is *not* the waiting-room. There isn't a waiting-room. A hospital this size what would we want a waiting-room for? This is the patients' lounge – for the up-patients. That's what they call them when they're up and moving around – just about ready to go home or maybe not much wrong with them in the first place. They can read or play cards, listen to the radio – anything they want. And naturally talk. Oh yes, plenty of books, a whole shelf, but just between ourselves they don't look very good. That's right, donated, we went around – ones people borrow and forget who's supposed to get them back. Somebody even gave a hymnbook and I think that's terrible. As if when you're sick in hospital you're not feeling bad enough already. . . . I'm not sure but I think they've got chequers and parchesi too. You know – games, for playing.

"No, I don't know what they wanted such a big lounge for either, but it'll at least give you a chance to get away by yourself in a corner. You know how it is when you've been sick yourself. The last thing you want to listen to is the terrible time somebody else has had. Anyway—

"The Gillespies donated the radio, all of them together – Dunc and Caroline and Sarah. A lovely gesture, don't you think? Oh yes, it comes in real loud.

"And Dr. Hunter, he gave the piano. His wife's – long before my time but they say she played just beautiful. We're not sure, though, about keeping it. It's fine for tonight because Benny Fox is coming to liven things up a bit – he's late – but what I mean supposing somebody starts playing and doesn't do it very well. There are plenty like that and they're always the ones. Just think if you were real sick say coming out of an operation and could hear somebody hammering away at *Though your sins be as scarlet.* Yes, I know *He will wash them white as snow,* but how can you be sure? And sick at your stomach and everything—

"Anyway, that's what we've decided – a lot more trouble than it's worth. Or say a youngster and *Chopsticks* – everybody wanting to wring its neck and a sick child or maybe its mother after all what can you do? Headaches, headaches, so just as soon as Doc's safely out of the way we're going to put an ad in the *Chronicle.* Two hundred, we think, at least to start with. The keys are getting sort of yellow and there's all that fancy stuff down the front but still it should be all right for learning on. That's right, somebody with children. It's a Mason and Risch and that's supposed to be the best. Or even a hundred and fifty – every dollar helps. There's a big loan to be paid off. No, I don't know how much exactly, it keeps going up and the government's mixed in somewhere but one thing for sure we're all going to be poor a long time paying taxes.... A lovely gesture though, don't you think?

"Oh no, the plants are just for tonight. They're ours – the Ladies' Auxiliary – we brought them. There was talk about ordering a couple of big baskets of roses and things but they cost so much and Doc's not what you'd call a flower man anyway. The big fern on the piano? That's mine – yes, I think so too. I put it up there so nobody'd knock into it. Oh my yes, I'd just die.

"Well now, this is *Reception* where you fill in forms and things – and pay. There's a couple of chairs so if for any reason you did have to wait then I suppose you could do it here. A hospital this size I don't see why but a car smash say and half a dozen lined up then in a case like that . . .

"Oh yes, I'm one of the Ladies Auxiliary – Assistant Secretary, I was voted in – and I don't mind telling you some of us are starting to wonder how much longer we can stand the strain. Sales and suppers, and making things. It's only six months since we started, and we've bought all the bedding and towels.... Yes, Mrs. Clarke, I understand your children are small but as you yourself say it's a good cause – maybe next year you'll be better organized. . . .

"Mrs. Gillespie Senior, Sarah, she's President – of the Auxiliary – and Dunc, he's President of the Board. Yes, all in the family – wonderful though to see a young man taking such an interest. Real community worker, on the School Board too. Well yes, I suppose it's good for business all right, although myself I'd never say it. After all some people are just born like that, a natural sense of public duty – I think that's what you call it. Caroline? Oh yes indeed. Right now she just comes but before long they'll be voting her in for something too, the President's wife, there's nothing surer.

"Well now, away we go. These two wheel chairs we've put them out in front just for tonight so people'll be sure to see. Donated, that's right, believe it or not by the Chinamen. Charlie Wong and Wing Ling Ching – or maybe it's the other way round, names like that how can you remember, one's got the restaurant and the other the laundry. Puts the rest of us to shame, now doesn't it? These things are dear you know and tonight I don't suppose they'll even come. Not just Wong and Wing but the others working with them, nine or ten all told – we've asked them specially but they're so shy. Anyway, we're leaving them out here in plain sight for everybody to see. That's right, it's not likely but there's no harm hoping. Lightning I always say myself never strikes the same place twice.

"Here now's the public ward – men, I think, although I don't suppose it makes much difference till they get them in – five beds and plenty of room to squeeze in a couple more if ever there's something going round – you know, an epidemic, say something in the water. Oh yes, they're real hospital beds. See – under here – there's a crank for up and down. You wind them. Right up-to-date – from Winnipeg."

"And women across the hall, five beds just the same. Nothing to see so away we go. Semi-private, private, just about the same too except what you pay. Myself unless I was real low I think I'd rather talk.

"Now the Operating Room – not much to see but they say it's where a lot of the money went. Everything locked up, all the knives and things. That's the table, though, where they lay you out and do it – like as not goes up and down too. Awfully narrow

– yes, that's what I think – I'd be scared of falling off but it's easier for them, I suppose, to get a grip. And anyway, I guess once you're this far you're not worrying, at least not for long. . . . Oh yes, the new doctor takes out things, appendixes and things – everything. Very good, they say, he's supposed to have learned it in the war.

"No, I don't remember him either but just between ourselves I'd as soon it was one of our own. I wouldn't carry on and make a fuss like some are doing but still I don't see why. You know, they've got their own way of looking at things, funny ideas, and now that we've got the hospital there must be plenty of nice young doctors like ourselves who'd be only too glad . . . Once a hunky always a hunky. Isn't it funny you say that. At the supper table tonight that's exactly what my husband said too. At least he ought to be starting out in a new place – exactly, not his old home town. Nick the Hunky – it's going to be awfully hard for people to forget.

"Anyway, let's go – the place gives me the creeps. You feel that way too? Starts you wondering what some day they'll be taking out of you. You read so much about it these days and now that we've got the hospital just wait and see – a couple of months it'll be all the rage.

"Here right next door's the Delivery Room. Not much to see either but before long it'll have some fine stories to tell too. Somebody's already booked in – Mrs. Ingram, you know, Mrs. Ted – and by the looks of things I wouldn't be surprised if she comes up with twins. Kind of nice in a way if she did, although it might scare others away. She's trying to hold on till Monday because the first one gets a prize – twenty-five dollars and a mug with its name on it for the baby. Yes, I guess that's right, we'd have to come across with two.

"Why Monday? Because that's when the matron and the nurses get here, and the new doctor too. Yes I know tonight's supposed to be the opening but the kitchen's not even ready, the men are still working, so they're just sort of making out it's the opening because it's Doc's birthday. Didn't you know? And it was his birthday the day he landed in Upward, that's right,

37

forty-five years ago today, so naturally they thought it would be a nice idea. . . . Well, if it makes him feel good what's the difference? In the meantime, Mrs. Ted's holding on.

"Well now, where are we? The Dispensary's locked and there's nothing much to see in X-rays so down we go to the kitchen. . . . Lovely, isn't it? Everything so clean. In a hospital naturally it's got to be clean but I mean it looks so clean – that's right, just shining. No, like I say it's not all connected up yet but a little later on we'll at least be able to have some coffee. Did you try the punch? Just terrible, I know, and such a shame for Doc's party – after all, you're seventy-five only once. Mrs. Grimble, she was the one. You see she's a member of the Auxiliary too and being the preacher's wife sort of gives her some say – nobody feels like talking back. Oh yes, temperance to the eyes. We did slip some gin and rum in, not enough to taste for anybody normal, but she's smacking her lips and saying 'Delicious, you see you don't *need* alcohol.' Anyway—

"There's going to be a cook and an assistant cook and a couple of maids and somebody to mop around. And an orderly – just one, though, for days; nights, I guess, you'll just have to keep on the right side of the nurse – and another man for the furnace and things. Laundry? No, Charlie Wong or Ling Wing Ching, whichever it is that has the laundry, he's looking after it, nurses' uniforms too. . . . You're telling *me* there's a lot of planning to do and things to think about. You never dream what you're running into till you get started. . . . Pots and pans and things, you don't want to look at them. An ambulance? Good Lord no, we're in the hole enough as it is, you'll just have to get here any way you can.

"Well, here we are again right back where we started. Thank you too, Mrs. Clarke, it's been a real pleasure. That's what we're here for – your hostesses. Three of us, taking turns. Have another glass of punch and don't forget we meet Fridays. Yes, I know it's hard when your children are small, my children are small too – but maybe next year, when you're better organized."

Hunky. And laugh. And sometimes I would too.

I was supposed to know better, people used to say you can count on Dunc he's serious he's reliable, when we were picking up sides for games everybody wanted to be on my side because I played fair and made everybody else play fair too, a couple of times I even got a prize at Sunday School and yet for all that I'd join in. Not often and not so mean as some of them, not like Stan and Ernie they were the worst they were always mean but just the same . . .

The shoes, that was one thing; thick and hard shoes, just one look and you knew they must hurt. But very strong, the kind that lasted. His father maybe thought he was being especially good to him making him such strong shoes, for in the country they came from that's what a shoemaker does is make shoes, he doesn't just put on new heels and soles. Sometimes the teacher would call him up to the blackboard clump clump just like a horse and the rest of us when we had to go up to the blackboard or maybe leave the room we'd go clump clump too. The one called Miss Gordon, with the red hair and purple dress . . . she was the one who used to yell.

His hair, that was another; hey Hunky, does your mother put a bowl on your head and then cut round? Fair very fair nearly white hair some days soaped down flat and some days crazy standing up like hay. That's what we used to say – it's his soap day or his hay day. And his father's pants cut down for him – something about the seat, you could always tell. What would he say would he mind I used to wonder if I gave him a pair of mine but still I'd join in. I'd call him Hunky too.

The shoe and harness shop was in front and the three of them lived behind. In one room. When you went with your shoes you never had a chance to see but the first thing was the smell. Sour milk and cabbage, garlic and leather, maybe other things – that kind of smell. In winter the door closed tight and a big fire going it would catch you by the throat. Hey Hunky, what do you eat in your place? Cabbage and cats? Mean little bastards – cabbage and cats, cabbage and cats – and sometimes I'd say it too. . . .

Then there was the cap, the funny fur cap that they must have brought with them – somebody maybe told them it was cold in Canada and they had it specially made, a very fine cap just right for thirty below and maybe his father thought he was being good to him, the same as with the strong boots, when he let him wear it. We used to fill it with snow and throw it like a ball, we'd take it from him and throw it to one another over his head. Where did you get the fur, Hunky? One of your cats?

When you went with your shoes there was always a cat, sometimes two, big fat sleepy ones the kind that purred, but they didn't eat or skin them. That was crazy, and mean. We knew they didn't. His father liked cats, that was all. They'd sit licking themselves and purring right beside him on the bench. Sometimes he'd say something to them in Ukrainian and they'd look up and mew back so it was their language too. When I was small that seemed a very strange thing, Canadian cats understanding Ukrainian.

A very small man but his wife was big. Big Anna, with the handkerchief and socks – so Nick took after her. He grew up tall with broad shoulders so it must have been after her.

A polite little man, fair like Nick – fair moustache too – and scared blue eyes. That was the first thing – very scared. And a scared smile when you opened the door, as if he was expecting something, something not good.

Nick was never scared. Sometimes he had to stay in four and five recesses in a row for fighting and sometimes when he fought it took three or four to hold him down. The day they were sitting on him and pulling his hair and opening his pants to take it out and spit on it and he bit Stanley's hand, that was the time I said no. I jumped in and punched Stanley. Four against one's not fair I said. You had it coming to you – good for Nick. Next time I hope he bites harder.

His English – that was another thing – *I von't, I vant, I not know do.* And the teacher with the purple dress she must have had other dresses too but it's always the purple one with the flaps I remember, the way she'd go sailing round the room cracking her ruler on the desks to make us sit up and listen and the flaps flying out like wings. She was the mean one, she'd stand him up in front to correct his English, pretending it was to help him, special attention, but what she wanted was a laugh. It was the old school in those days, only two rooms; the other three or four grades, not just ours, would all stop what they were doing and listen too. He hadn't learned English before he started school, only a few words, because he was a hunky – it had started away back even then. He had no neighbours; other little kids if they saw him on the street would throw things or make faces and run. So instead of going out to play he stayed home all day with his father, cutting up scraps of leather and talking Ukrainian to the cats.

We called Benny names too. Worse names. Mamma's pet – that was a polite one. Taking turns: hey Benny, do you sit down to pee? Nick because of the big boots and the fur cap and the smell, and Benny because his mother sent him to school – at least till the day she took too many pills – all dressed up in his best clothes as if he was going to Sunday School. Only worse – collar and bow tie and in summer a boater, sometimes even white pants and a blue jacket and the rest of us in overalls. Because we were all against them both Benny seemed to think they should stand together and be friends – always trailing him, trying to keep close and squeeze in – I suppose he thought that then they would at least each have one, but it takes two to keep close and Nick didn't want Benny. He didn't want anybody. He didn't want me.

That was ten. About ten. Sometimes when I had a chocolate bar I would give him half. Divide it fair, the way I always had to divide things fair with Stanley, and then I'd slip it to him so nobody would see. I wanted to be friends but I didn't want anybody else to know I was being friends. Later, yes, I stood up to them, but not then. So it was always when we were alone, on the sly. And he knew. He was sharp, saw through you fast, so he must have known. And he must have had names in Ukrainian for me too.

He'd take the chocolate and eat it fast, a gulp, and then look to see if there was more. Never thanks. Like a dog beside you at the table, sitting close and swallowing fast when you slip it something, fast so as to be ready for the next bit, swallowing and thumping its tail and maybe even whining to make sure you know it's still there. That sometimes bothered me. I'd give him the piece of chocolate – not always chocolate, sometimes I'd have an apple to divide, or two plums or two sticks of gum – to let him see I wanted to be friends, that I wasn't like the others, not like Stan and Ernie, but so far as he was concerned we were all the same. At least close enough. If I wanted to be friends it was up to me. Strong, just like the boots. We put him and Benny on the same side, the other side, together, but they weren't on the same side. Not because Nick was ashamed of Benny, of being known as his friend like I was ashamed of being known as Nick's friend, but because he was strictly on his own side.

The piece of chocolate or the plum – he cared just about that. While I was in the mood, willing. Hay while the sun shines. I might change again. Why say thanks? We called him Hunky, fought him four to one and threw his cap. All of us. I threw it too. We were his enemies.

The same – a little later, eleven, twelve – when Doc started taking us with him on calls, first for a while just me, then Nick too. I didn't mind, I tried being even friendlier to show I didn't mind but he didn't care whether I minded or not. It was Doc's car, not mine. And Doc had asked him.

For the ride. To open gates. To have somebody to talk to. To show us things. (But first it had been just to show me things.) Saturdays and Sundays and sometimes after school. Depending how late it was and how far. Sometimes in summer when there was no school. But I couldn't count on it. Neither could Nick. Hanging around his gate waiting to be asked was no good. If it wasn't the right day he'd just say Hi Dunc and drive off – he was like that. Once I wasn't supposed to go, it was Saturday, and Saturday when the store was busy I had work to do, but I went anyway because I knew Nick would be going and I didn't want to be left out. Father was jumping and said next time I'd get my ass kicked in. And to make up for it I had to work after school a whole week.

The first few weeks, when I was the only one, it made me important, the most important boy in school. Even more impor-

42

tant than the older boys, three or fours years older. He let me watch him doing things, like the time he sewed up the boy who'd fallen and cut his wrist on a saw, explaining, very serious, how important it was to keep things clean so the germs wouldn't get in, how sometimes they got in anyway. That was why he had a pan of boiling water, to sterilize the needle. Washing his hands as he talked, something stronger than soap, a long time, explaining that was why I couldn't help him, couldn't hand him things.

I talked about it at school and somebody told the teacher, not the redheaded one with the purple flaps, a good one, and she had me come up to the front and tell the whole room. That day I was the hygiene lesson. Everybody listened. For a few days they were all calling me Doc.

And to myself I started thinking maybe when I grew up I would go to college and be a real doctor.

At first when Doc started taking Nick too I thought it was just because he knew about the bad time he had at school and wanted to make it up to him, so he wouldn't feel out of things. But that wasn't why. A few times and I began to see. Nick was the one. He talked more to him than to me and he spent more time explaining things. He still talked and made jokes with me too, sometimes catching himself talking so much to Nick and starting in fast to talk to both of us, but then he'd forget again, he couldn't help it, it was the way things were – the way we were. He used to try not to let it show. One of these days you're going to end up a fine pair of doctors, he'd say – but Nick was the one.

The time the woman was all ready to have her baby and Nick wanted to watch – that was when I understood. Crazy Hunky, I sat thinking, a woman having her baby of all things and wanting to watch, don't you know anything? waiting for Doc to jump on him and tell him off, but instead, serious, he said he was sorry, he'd like him to see it, it would be good for him, but at a time like that a woman wanted only another woman and the doctor. "You'll have to wait," he said, "till you're an intern in a hospital or at least a student, but don't worry, there's plenty to see and learn about in the meantime."

Meaning it. Meaning every word of it. Just as if it was all

settled and arranged. Nick the Hunky going to be a doctor. His mother with the black handkerchief, scrubbing around town at fifteen cents an hour. Was Doc crazy? Didn't he know?

But a few days and it was all right again. Nick was the one; and I didn't mind. I got over it. I was still on his side. Before, I'd slipped him chocolate on the sly, wanting to make it up to him for calling him Hunky but not wanting anybody to know. But now I was on his side and I wanted everybody to know.

Eleven, twelve – things were changing. He spoke English like the rest of us – even better. Once that was what one of the teachers said, it wasn't his language yet he spoke it better than we did and we ought to be ashamed. He didn't say 'I should of went' he said 'I should have gone.' So there were no more easy laughs. And he'd got rid of the cap and was wearing pants and shoes like the rest of us. He even went to the barbershop for Sammy Fox to cut his hair.

Twelve, thirteen – in there. About the time his father went to the sanitarium in Fort Qu'Appelle and died. There was no more harness shop but they still lived there. His mother still scrubbed and washed around town; that was how they got by. I was still trying to be his friend, sitting beside him every chance and going places together and sharing things, and he was still just not minding. Up to me – if I wanted to. He always let it show. I was his friend but he wasn't mine. He didn't trust us, not even Benny.

By that time Benny's mother was dead too. Because people talked. Because Benny had come when she was married six or seven months and they never let her forget. And then after she did it – at least people said she did it, she took the whole bottle – it was easier for Benny because his father had sense enough not to make him wear the bow ties. He sold the house and they went to live just the two of them over the barbershop. A little easier, but too late. We still laughed. We were still little bastards. For his clothes had changed but he hadn't. We made fun of him – his voice, and the polite way he did things for the teacher. Still like a little girl, he couldn't help it. Sometimes when we laughed he would even cry. Nick never laughed, never joined in, but he didn't takes sides or make friends with him either. Still going his own way. An eye peeled. Alone – even when I was with him he was alone. First we made him that way. Then that was the way he wanted it.

I didn't even know when he left town. Right after his mother died: everybody was surprised, she looked so big and strong, and then one day hanging out somebody's washing it was all over in a quarter of an hour. He'd got ahead of me a year by then and had just finished High School, Grade Eleven, so he must have been fifteen. I went to the funeral, Mother too. They didn't belong to the Church but the preacher said since they were Christians, even though not the right kind, she mustn't be buried without a service and some prayers. Mother said bring him home for a few days, I can't bear to think of him going back to that grubby little place alone, we'll have to do something, but he just looked at me and said no, Doc was looking after things. The next few days I kept watching for him and wondering. It was a week before I knew he'd gone.

Just picked up and left. The beds and chairs and dishes and things, he just walked off and left them. Not many things, not very good, not enough for an auction sale. Doc was still in charge. Charlie Wong took some for the restaurant and the rest just stayed there. Till they tore down the building; then they must have thrown them out. It wasn't their building, they rented it, but nobody else moved in. Sometimes when I was passing I would stop a minute and look at the old green blind and wonder how he was doing. Once I caught myself thinking about the smell – was it still there? Then another day the window was soaped over – just as if it had caught me trying to look in.

For a long time I didn't ask Doc. I didn't like to – he seemed to think I knew. Then at last I said ever hear from Nick and he said oh yes, he's fine, he's with a Ukrainian family in Winnipeg. I wasn't going on calls with him by that time because I was fifteen, sixteen, catching up at school and working in the store. A lot of times I'd forget all about Nick and then I'd be passing and happen to look up and there would be the little soap-eyed window.

But I'm the one now. It's come round. I'm the one bringing him back. If it wasn't for me . . . Yes, Doc knew all about him, where he was, he'd been keeping track, but I was the one who wrote and said why don't you? President of the Board – I beat down all the rest of the Board. And it's going to be all right – he's changed or he wouldn't be coming, he wouldn't have said yes. Coming because he wants to come. Coming back where he belongs.

"Hi Benny, we were starting to think you'd forgotten us. Have some punch, it's terrible, but just a quick one. We're waiting – you've got work to do. The place is like a funeral parlour."

"Yes Benny, everybody's got such a long face. Not too loud, but something bright and cheerful."

"Sorry I'm late – hello Caroline – but we play tomorrow and simply had to have a run-through. Stan's gone home to change – he'll be along in half an hour."

"Stan's not planning to sing?"

"Well yes – why not? We thought *Among My Souvenirs.*"

"Good God no, this is Doc's party and if there's one thing he can do without it's Stan singing *Among My Souvenirs.*"

"Well then, excuse *me*! Since the President of the Board has decided that music is *not* in order, far be it from me to spoil his little evening for him."

"Benny, we do want music, we just don't want Stan and *Among My Souvenirs.*"

"No no, not for anything in the world. I'm going to shake hands with Doc and wish him well and then I'll be on my way. So sorry to have alarmed you."

"Benny don't be such a damned fool. If we didn't want you to play we wouldn't have asked you."

"Yes Benny, just to break the chill."

"When you were planning things, Mr. President, why didn't you stop to think it would be like a funeral parlour? And get some advice? Even the way you've arranged the chairs, in rows, all at one end and poor Doc at the other, as if he was going to give a talk on venereal disease or the joys of breast feeding. Where did you get the chairs? Raid the church?"

"Where else? The basement – the ones for Sunday School. We thought people would wander around more talking and just sit down when they were tired but they're not wandering."

"You see, Benny, we don't want him on his feet all evening. He's going to be tired enough as it is, the presentation's not till half-past ten. So that means he can talk to only two or three at a time."

"We wanted stronger punch but somebody never mind who put her firm little foot down and said nothing alcoholic."

"And why don't you stand up to them? You're the President, aren't you? You're not backward about standing up to Stan and me."

"Be a good boy, Benny – *Bye-Bye Blackbird* and *My Blue Heaven* – they'll be just right to start with."

"You see, if Stan sings everybody will have to be polite and listen – it'll turn into a concert. Doc too – he'll have to be polite; and then of course everybody will clap. But they won't know how much – enough to keep things friendly and pleasant but not enough to make him think they want another."

"I never listened to anything so ridiculous in my life. So childish, just because you're his brother."

"Stanley has such a loud voice, Benny. It's all right to belt it out – is that the way you say it? – when he's singing with the band, but tonight we just want a little background music, to help people relax."

"And how's Stan going to feel? And how do you think I feel? I suggested it. He's been practising."

"The trouble is I've already turned Mrs. Billy down – she was in the store this morning wondering if an old song like *The End of a Perfect Day* wouldn't be a good way to round out the evening – because if I'd said yes to her I'd have had to ask Mrs. Jack too and she'd have wanted to sing *The Lost Chord*. Well then, if Stan gets up to sing there'll be all hell to pay. He's my brother and I'm the President—"

"Indeed you are and doing a simply marvellous job! No no, I'm not getting mixed up in your sordid little squabbles. I'll just shake hands and run along. So sorry."

"Something else, Benny – it's Doc's piano."

"What's that got to do with it?"

"Well, I think it might please him – make him think we're grateful, that a piano's just what we want."

"Be a good boy, Benny – *Bye-Bye Blackbird*—"

"All right, Caroline, for you – strictly for you – but later on just the same I may have a little surprise for you. I've just thought of it. Stan and Mrs. Billy and Mrs. Jack, I'll get them all to sing – together. We'll ask Doc if there's an old one—"

"Easy, easy. Mrs. Billy and Mrs. Jack haven't spoken to each other for the last ten years. We don't want a hair-pulling contest."

"Look Rose, there's Benny – I think he's going to play. Oh I hope so – everybody's looking so mournful."

"Yes, he's winding down the stool. . . . You know, Nellie, it's funny, but it doesn't seem very long ago he always had to wind it up. For a while they had him playing the hymns for Sunday School, I was one of the teachers, and I remember he used to sit up so nice and straight. . . . And now just look at the shoulders, the way he slumps. It makes him look so old, and he can't be much more than thirty."

"More like his mother every day, now that at long last he's starting to lose the little boy look. Something about the mouth —"

"I know, mouth and eyes, a pinched look. I suppose she suffered, poor soul, more than any of us knew."

"Well, it was her own doing. She brought it on herself."

"That's harsh, Nellie. She was here all alone, remember, without her mother."

"And I don't just mean because she let Sam Fox talk her off

the straight and narrow. He did the right thing by her. She was a respectable married woman just like the rest of us. She had the right to hold her head just as high. It was the grand way she tried holding it higher, talking down to everybody – and the way she took it out on poor Benny and Sam."

"Nobody *knows*, Nellie, that she took it out on Benny."

"You only needed your eyes – the way she used to dress him. The bow ties and the boater – not just as good as the other little boys who took nine months to make it instead of five, but oh dear me so much better. We came to Upward when he was about five and long after that, a couple of years at least, she used to rig him out so help me in a sailor suit with a ribbon down his back – that's right, a ribbon – you must have seen it too. And the scared, lost look. I daresay she used to warn him what would happen if he got his pretty suit dirty or dared play rough with the other boys."

"Well, I suppose it was knowing how people talk, the humiliation. They say she came from a very good family."

"*She* said she came from a good family. What's a good family anyway? If you're really somebody it shows – that's what Dan always says. You don't have to go round trying to impress people."

"Do you suppose, Nellie, that's why?"

"Why what?"

"The bow ties and things, never letting him have fun with the other boys or get into fights – do you suppose it made him turn?"

"Well, she and Sam were certainly normal enough – at least judging by the fix they got themselves into – so he didn't inherit it."

"And he's really such a nice boy, and he does play beautifully. Just listen – *Bye-Bye Blackbird*—"

"You're getting your birds mixed, aren't you? That's *When the Red Red Robin Comes a Bob-Bob-Bobbin'.*"

"Don't laugh at me, Nellie. I know they like each other instead of us, but just what is it exactly that they *do?*"

"Well, I don't know *exactly* what they do, Rose, but stop and think a minute how they're made. What *can* they do?"

"Well, as you can see for yourself, Mrs. Caine, he's got three talking to him already. Why don't you just relax and listen to the music?"

"Yes, if I'd only known Benny would be playing I'd have brought my Joey. He just worships the ground he walks on."

"Does he? Joey, if I remember right, is the one who wants to play the piano too?"

"Oh yes, nights there's a dance I have a terrible time with him. He slips out on me and goes down to the hall to listen. They let him in free – depending on who's at the door. At thirteen he's naturally not there to dance."

"Well, it's certainly a wonderful way for a thirteen-year-old boy to spend his time – at the piano, I mean, not with Benny – but if he's so crazy about music shouldn't he be taking some lessons?"

"Just as soon as we get a piano – we think this Christmas."

"Do you like this one?"

"Oh yes, if only I'd brought Joey. There now, he's starting *Jealousy* – it's a tango. He knows them all, he's always whistling."

"Do you like the tone, Mrs. Caine?"

"Oh yes, Benny's got a lovely touch."

"Not Benny, the piano—"

"Very nice, it sort of rings."

"Dr. Hunter's donated it – a lovely gesture, don't you think? They say his wife was a beautiful musician."

"And I suppose he just couldn't bring himself to sell it. Now wasn't that nice of him! I'm sure it will bring a lot of happiness."

"Well, what we're hoping it will bring is a little cash. After all a hospital's not the place. As I was saying just a while ago, it's always the ones that can't play that keep trying – nothing to drive you up the wall faster."

"Oh dear, you mean—"

"Yes, at first that's how I felt too, but we've got to be practical."

"And poor Dr. Hunter—"

"He'll be in Saskatoon. Two hundred we think – for the Hospital Aid Fund."

"It seems such a shame – I'm sure he meant well."

"We're putting an ad in the *Chronicle* next week – just as soon as he's safely out of the way. I know at least three who'll be interested but on account of your Joey being so musical I thought you might like to have the first chance."

"I see. Well, all along we've had in mind a new piano. That's why we've been holding off so long."

"It would do for a year or two. Joey's not getting any younger."

"But you know how it is – when you get something to do for a year or two it keeps on doing."

"You say yourself it's got a lovely tone. And a very handsome instrument."

"Yes, for a hospital."

"Well, if it's handsome it's handsome. What's the hospital got to do with it?"

"I mean a piano in a waiting-room is one thing and the same piano in your own home is something else again."

"This is a lounge, Mrs. Caine – for patients when they're getting better."

"You know what I mean. A hundred did you say?"

"*Two* hundred – and a bargain. It hasn't got a scratch."

"If it belonged to his wife it must go back a long way. Two hundred for such an old one seems a lot."

"I've always heard they made them better in the old days. It's a lost art."

"Styles change, though – and it's so big. It seems to me a hundred would be plenty."

"It's a Mason and Risch. That's supposed to be the best."

"My sister has a Heintzman – the one in Medicine Hat."

"Well, your sister's Heintzman in Medicine Hat isn't much help to Joey in Upward, now is it?"

"It's just that I've always heard a Heintzman is the best. A hundred I suppose would be a bargain."

"It certainly would. We're asking two. And you keep saying it's got such a lovely tone."

"Yes, when Benny's playing."

"Well, the sooner Joey gets started the sooner he'll have a lovely tone too. Already he's away behind. They say Benny could play *The Maple Leaf Forever* when he was seven. Standing to attention."

"Oh dear – since he's so far behind anyway I suppose a few more months won't make much difference. I'll talk it over with my husband but in the meantime you'd better go ahead and run your ad."

"Perhaps Mrs. Gillespie you'll be good enough to tell me just what's going on. Now I hear you know the new doctor too."

"I don't exactly know him, Mrs. Harp. I met him, just for a minute, and so far as I know nothing's going on."

"Well, it's very strange. Doc Hunter knows all about him, Dunc knows all about him, and now I hear you're in on it too. You see what I mean – the rest of us who've got to foot the bills we're all in the dark. You're from away over in England – how come he's a friend of yours too?"

"He's Duncan's friend – as I'm sure you know they went to school together – and I hope he'll be my friend too. What's so strange? I met him in the hospital."

"It just seems funny. You're new in town, you might say a stranger, and yet you know more about him than the oldtimers. Dunc goes off to the Army and brings you back, then he brings Nick back, then it turns out you know Nick too."

"We just shook hands, Mrs. Harp. He was passing through the ward."

"Away over in England? Doesn't it seem a funny coincidence?"

"No, he was in the Canadian Army so it's hardly surprising that he was attached to a Canadian hospital. Duncan was wounded and in the same hospital – that's the only coincidence. And I was visiting Duncan. We'd met a few months before and I already had designs on him."

"I suppose so. It's just that some of us, Mrs. Gillespie – and I don't see any reason for being backward about saying so – are not at all happy the way things are turning out. We've waited for years to build this hospital, and now, when at last it's ready, somebody like him comes along to take over."

"They say he's very good. Duncan told me that in the hospital there were a great many stories about him, all the right kind. At that time he wasn't thirty, and doing wonderful things. And since then I think he's spent a year in Boston."

"If you'd known him, Mrs. Gillespie, when we did. If you'd seen his mother—"

"I wouldn't be surprised if you like him. As I say, it was only a minute or two – Duncan called him over and introduced us – but he gave the impression of being a very serious, rather nice young man. Shy, tall – what else? Blue eyes, I think, high cheekbones, very fair—"

"If he's so good what's he coming back to Upward for? I know why – to take it out on us, to show who he is now."

"Oh no, I'm sure that's not how he feels. In fact that was one of the things that impressed me. I remember thinking aren't Canadians wonderful? He was an officer, a captain, and he was walking through the ward with another captain and a major, and Duncan, just a sergeant, shouted 'Hi Nick, come over here, I want you to meet somebody' and he came."

"And what's wonderful about that?"

"Well, if an English sergeant called an officer by his first name, especially in the presence of other officers, he'd be in for it. At least a very sharp reprimand. I'm sure he would never do it again."

"And what would he call him?"

"Well, an officer is addressed as 'Sir.'"

"A hunky like Nick? Don't make me laugh!"

"Yes, Mrs. Harp, in the Canadian Army too."

"Then good for Dunc that he didn't. Army or no Army, captain or doctor or whatever else you want to call him – good for Dunc that he had the guts to stand up to him."

"No, no, he wasn't standing up to him. He didn't call him Nick to bring him down a peg, or at least to try to bring him down. That was the last thing on his mind. He called him Nick because they were old friends and that's what I thought was so wonderful, that the friendship should cut through rank and leave no scars."

"His mother, Mrs. Gillespie, used to wash for my mother. Big Anna. She wore a black handkerchief and red socks. She couldn't even speak English; she just used to grunt. How do you think the women of this town are going to feel about discussing things with her son – intimate things?"

"It seems to me you should be very proud. After all, isn't he an Upward boy? Didn't Upward help make him?"

"You've got a lot to learn, Mrs. Gillespie. It's not hard to see you've never known a hunky."

"He won't last long, just mark my words. The last six months – haven't you noticed? He used to be so sharp and spry and all at once he's old. And going off like this to live in Saskatoon – a niece of all things, a widow."

"Very quiet, they say, the dumpy kind. Somebody he can order around, you can be sure of that. She was here for a few days last fall, I suppose to talk things over, but she didn't go out much. Very religious, according to Mrs. Green."

"Just the two of them they'll drive each other crazy."

"And he could have such a good time here, all his old friends. Old Harry Hubbs – they could play poker."

"But he wouldn't be the doctor any more. New hospital, new young fellow looking after things – he's been the big frog too long."

"Mrs. Green could just carry on. She knows his ways. With your own it never works – far better among strangers."

"Pride, I suppose – everybody saying poor old Doc."

"Within the year. You mark my words."

After all what did I expect him to do, sit down and hold my hand? The nurses said sometimes eighteen hours a day they were flying them back by the planeload, it was at the very worst and I was just another. And he did stop sometimes, he asked about Stan and how was the store coming along, little things like that he remembered and I wasn't even his patient he hadn't been the one but still he'd take a minute sometimes to look at my chart and say it shouldn't be long. Fourteen fifteen years was there supposed to be a celebration just because we'd gone to school together?

Things had happened for him and they hadn't for me, that was what I kept forgetting. I was where I was when he left Upward just fifteen years older still Dunc the grocery boy while he had been busy, changes, jumps, a lot of bad times too there must have been all through the depression years – things on his mind, problems and work, much more important things.

Maybe if it hadn't been for the 'captain' – it mattered to some of them, there were the pricks that liked it but this was different years and years we'd known each other I called him Nick because it seemed right because I was afraid if I said Captain or Sir he would think I was being snotty, sarcastic, my way of reminding him of the fur cap and the harness shop—

No, I'm making that up – the first time I saw him I didn't think at all, about fur caps or being snotty or anything else, I yelled Nick because I was so excited, we were so far away and

I was so glad, just the sight of him, somebody I knew. A nurse came running thinking I'd gone off my head trying to get out of bed and then after starting how could I go back and say Sir?

Not that it mattered to him he had other things so many shot up and dying he wasn't the kind anyway but still it was in the way. It spoiled things. Not much, because he was always in a hurry and there wasn't much to spoil, but a little. When he came into the ward I'd try to catch his eye and then just grin or wave, not calling him anything, and I'd be careful again when he came over to the bed. The time with Caroline—

"Good evening Mrs. Leckie, how are you Fred – we were afraid with the roads so slippery not many from the country would get in. That's right, winter always hates to go – a few sunny days and then it freezes again – one way or another we always get our five months. Here comes my wife, she'll give you some punch. Doc's going to be awfully pleased—"

The time with Caroline I forgot again. Nick I yelled just like the first time excited again and proud wanting him to meet her wanting to show her off afraid he'd get away, Hi Nick and he looked surprised and the other two he was with looked surprised too but still he came. It was all right, he didn't mind. Surprised, that was all, a look on his face, not minding but thinking maybe what the hell Dunc ought to have more sense. Friendly, shook hands – what more could he do and the other two waiting and watching with what-the-hell looks too? Not just to meet her but to talk that was what I wanted, a few minutes for him to see. I wanted to say maybe an evening together the three of us she's special very special you'll see not the good-time kind we'll have dinner and see a show anything you like, I wanted to tell him how I had met her at a show wanted them to talk together I was so proud—

And proud of him too, yes, that was part of it, wanted her to know that in Upward they weren't all horses big and dumb like me. Even though he'd left a long time ago and didn't belong there any more still I thought maybe I could use him so she would think this Upward can't be such a terrible place – that's right, wanted to use him, Nick the Hunky with the clump clump boots and the hair like hay.

But every time before I could speak up he was away again, always running, new ones coming in every day so many they were putting beds in the corridors. Every time when he stopped for a minute going through instead of asking I'd go tight and cold and then it would be too late again. Right to the last morning in a hurry again be back later he called and then the jeep was waiting and I didn't see him again—

"Yes, Mrs. Billy, you're a hundred per cent right, it's not a very lively party and the place isn't exactly jumping, but the important thing after all is giving Doc a chance to chat with his old friends. And he's seventy-five – can you give me one good reason why the place should be jumping?"

"What I'd like to know is how. Right through the bad years, everybody flat broke – I can remember when a tin of pork and beans was living high, a Sunday treat – and he ends up a doctor."

"They do things a white man wouldn't, that's how. Same as the Chinks – live on anything, live like pigs – it doesn't bother them. And summers I suppose he'd find a job."

"But there were no jobs. He left just when things were starting to get tight, he must have been fifteen."

"They stick together, cousins, friends, half a dozen to a room, three to a bed. Somebody I suppose would let him bunk in and give him a bowl of cabbage soup."

"You wonder, though. You don't get through Medical School on a bowl of cabbage soup. I suppose he's got a lot of credit coming."

"Credit or not, there should have been a vote – for everybody. Dunc and some of them on the Board like old Dan Furby take too much on themselves. It's our hospital. People with wives and families – we're the ones."

"Well, I've got no special love for hunkies either, but after all we brought them in. They've got a right to a chance same as anybody else. I say so long as he does the job."

"We didn't bring them in to take over and go to college. How's your wife going to feel if she gets sick and has to tell him things – maybe about her and you? Or take off her clothes for an examination? They've got funny minds and don't fool yourself, he's still a hunky. It would take a lot more than Medical School."

"One at a time they're all right. They even try harder, sort of fall over backwards trying not to let it show."

"I say somebody ought to step in fast. This has always been a white town."

"And it'll stay white. He's smart enough to know nobody's forgotten. He'll be a good case of falling over backwards just to make sure."

"But we don't want somebody falling over backwards to show he's white. We want real white, one of our own."

"Supposed to have been good in the war."

"So what? Working on somebody that's been shot up and hasn't much chance of making it anyway, that's not the same as a straight job of curing."

"Doc's no fool you know and they say he did a lot of checking. Wrote a lot of letters – he'd know the places."

"He's seventy-five. The last couple of years he's been going round in a fog. Look at him right now, nodding and mumbling away like an old owl – no idea what it's all about. Dunc's the one."

"You've got to hand it to Dunc just the same. He's been working hard for the hospital – a good man for the town."

"Another couple of years he'll be changing the name from Upward to Gillespie if someone doesn't trip him up. Big ideas about himself, ever since he came back with his medal and his fancy English bride. People scared to talk back to him – grocery bill not paid, and going to need more. Old Dan's a good example – a quarter-page advertisement in his famous *Chronicle* every week. I suppose it keeps him and Nellie eating."

"You know what this town needs right now? A Jew – to smarten people up a little."

"Like a hole in the head we need a Jew. That's one thing so far we've been lucky."

"No, one at a time they're fine, same as the hunkies. And good competition – just what Dunc needs."

"But it's the way they do things – no principles. They say they've just about taken over Comet."

"Not one at a time. Look at the Chinks – they're all right even six or seven at a time. Just because they're not white they try extra hard. Didn't you see the chairs?"

"What chairs?"

"The wheel chairs – two of them. Over there behind old Sarah Gillespie. Keeping on the right side of us. Anybody else making donations like that?"

"Chinks are different – polite and easy, keeping out of things. Hunkies and Jews mean trouble."

"Not one at a time. Our old friend Nick won't just stop at being white. He'll bleach himself."

"Hello Sarah, I see a faraway look in your eyes – lots of memories, I suppose?"

"As a matter of fact, Nellie, I've been sitting here thinking about the time I had to take down my pants and bend over for him, I must have been twelve, so he could look at my ringworms and dab on iodine. That's right – ringworms. Two big red beauties, one on each cheek, just like doughnuts."

"Lucky you! He never asked me to take down my pants and bend over so he could see how my cheeks were doing."

"Yes, but they were such big cheeks, even away back then, and it was just the time I was having such a head-over-heels affair with him. Handsome young doctor from down east, always dressed up in his Sunday suit, collar and tie. Talk about a crush! I used to lie awake at night thinking up ways to get rid of his wife – poor Edith! – and then away we'd go on our honeymoon to Swift Current or Moose Jaw and eat ice cream and gingerbread for breakfast. Oh yes, he insisted – nothing was too good for me."

"Well, I've often said to myself the House of Gillespie just can't be the model of propriety and Christian rectitude it seems. There must be at least one black sheep grazing in the shadows, but I never dreamed it would turn out to be you. Does Duncan know about his mother's flighty past?"

"Poor Dunc – he'd die rather than show it, but I think he's all in knots these days. Ever since he was a little fellow Doc's meant so much to him, he's always looked up to him so. Saying good-bye is like saying good-bye to a part of himself. And at the same time he's so excited about the new hospital and Nick coming back to take over – *our* Nick, he calls him."

"And that's just about what Dan's saying in the *Chronicle:* the hospital's a milestone, we've turned a corner. How does he put it – 'It's a red-letter day for Upward and it's also a very sad day. There's pride in our hearts, a sense of achievement, new faith in the future, and there's also the tug of memories—' And then something about a kind of loneliness, a hollow place, as we think of all we've lost, all the good, brave years that lie behind us."

"Maybe it isn't that we've actually lost so much, Nellie, as that in the old days we were younger, everything seemed within reach. That's what made them the good old days. We were looking ahead, there was a bigger sky."

"We've been here only twenty-seven years yet it's the same. We didn't come to Saskatchewan, to a town called Upward. Oh no, indeed we didn't, we came West. We wanted more sky too. But here we are just the same bedded down in Upward with our six-page *Chronicle.* New hospital, new doctor, new sidewalks. Next year if things work out Dan should even have his new press, but it will still be the *Chronicle.* Eight pages instead of six – more space for ads."

"Have you ever looked up Main Street, Nellie, and wondered how in Heaven's name we all got here – what made us decide, or at least what made our parents decide? The Chinamen, old Harry Hubbs. Years ago, maybe before your time, there was an old music teacher called Phyllis Devine with a red wig and a little fox fur. She always wore it for her pupils. And the hunkies – our Nick – why did they get off the train *here,* who told them, what did they expect to find?"

"Big Anna and little John – such hard, wasted lives."

"Only Nick – and not even to know."

"Tonight they'd be so proud . . . But I mustn't sit here chattering, Sarah – the *Chronicle* calls. Notes for my *Nosey Parker* column. I've neglected it this week so it's time to get on with my snooping. I'm so glad you gave me the little story about the ringworms. I'll put it first."

"Now Nellie, that's not fair—"

He looks so tired and lost, that one little tuft God help us standing up pure white – and there used to be so much of it so black and thick—

Curly, with a shine, not like poor Father's sandy licks and the bald spot starting to show. Shaved too, always shaved, and always in his Sunday suit just like the pictures in the Men's Clothes Section of Eaton's catalogue, at least I thought it was his Sunday suit and that he put it on because he was coming to see us, special, an occasion, but Mother said oh no, doctors aren't like farmers they shave and put a tie on every day, and laughed, big joke, nearly splitting herself – she told him – and after all it wasn't my fault I was such a know-nothing little country girl she had a lot more to do with it than I did. Laugh laugh she loved a laugh when it was at somebody else's expense, especially at her own dear daughter Sarah's expense. Remember now and call him Dr. Hunter, speak up like a little lady but don't hang around and stare there's nothing worse, just how do you do and then run along and play.

The first time – it couldn't really have been the first time but the first time I remember, the first time he became important to me, a man in my life, I was eleven, about eleven, at least it was before the ringworms and that was twelve, the first time was the day he let me carry in the robe. A buffalo robe, twenty years if it's a day since I've seen one, brown and curly a very dark brown nearly black with a red lining, scarlet, that kind of red and scalloped edges, such swank – ours, we had one too, was mangy and old, it wasn't just for keeping warm with in the sleigh, we used it as a horse blanket sometimes for wrapping up a sick calf warm and furry just the thing but this one, his, was strictly for the knees. Soft and curly something like his hair it even had a special smell and that day, the first day, so it would be warm for him when it was time to go, he let me carry it in from the cutter to the kitchen. I carried the robe while he came along behind with the foot warmer.

There were bricks, black bricks, something like bricks, he called them bricks – you put them in the oven to get hot and then when you were ready to go you put them in the foot warmer then you put your feet on the foot warmer and that way for an hour or two you had warm feet. At least he had warm feet. We didn't have a foot warmer, when our feet got cold we jumped out and ran. There must have been other times because we seemed to know each other, I called him Dr. Hunter and he called me Sarah, and some of the things I remember about him must have come before but still it was the first time. I carried the robe while he followed with the foot warmer and from that day on there was a man in my life.

There were long waits, at least they seemed long, and yet he came often. Why? We were never sick – almost never. When he was out our way, Happy Haven way, going somewhere on a call, he would drive in for a glass of buttermilk or to water his horse and if he stayed for a meal we had salmon and preserved strawberries. A tin always on the shelf specially for him in case there wasn't anything else except salt pork, and even a big tin not being very big she'd spin it out with lettuce and hard-boiled eggs. Whatever I did, standing orders, I wasn't to ask for more, I could make up on potatoes and pickles afterwards. Once something got into her and instead of using me as a joke she said Sarah picked the strawberries, wild ones in the pasture, and he winked and said I was a good picker. Lights, stars, what a day.

But sometimes, so it wasn't always salmon, she'd say stop in on your way back and I'll have a chicken. She hated killing a chicken and usually such a fuss – something for a man to do he ought to take out the insides too we didn't have chickens in Owen

Sound I wasn't brought up that way – but not a word when it was a chicken for the doctor. Poor Father, sometimes I wonder. And the way she'd send me out to make kindling and look for eggs.

The first day, though, when it all started, that day I don't remember what we ate – it was winter so maybe stew or steak; we used to kill a steer and keep it frozen in one of the granaries – not even what we had for dessert, because carrying in the robe and spreading it on two chairs beside the stove so that to the last curl it would be warm for him and then sitting back with my eyes shut while he tucked it round my knees, that for one day was enough to remember.

His knees, too, and away we went flying along in the red cutter with the bays kicking up snow and the bells chinging and the foot warmer keeping our feet warm while the neighbours ran to doors and windows quick quick it's Dr. Hunter and look who's with him will you, if it isn't Sarah Robinson, he must be taking her to town—

The first of many trips to town, many rides with the bays – that was the way I went to sleep now. A wife, unfortunately yes, and living as we were in a world permitting only one I had no alternative, so straight for the jugular, just like a chicken's neck, one good hard chop and get it over with. Considering my years and inexperience the runaway not a bad first try, the bays understandably on edge the haughty way she twirled her parasol; a trial run or two, though, and I found myself squeamish at the spatter of blood and brains. Something to be said too for the poison, poking among his bottles and things she had it coming to her – so what if she did have a stomach ache she could have waited – but it was nearly as bad as the shattered skull the way she writhed and then turned green. Well, try try and try again the best of us must learn and after all since it was something I was going to have to live with why not just let her slowly waste away? Time for me to meet her and for a bond to grow, so that towards the end, cool hand on fevered brow, my rightful place was at her side. At his side too, comforting and sustaining, inspiring him with hope. My own dear Sarah, if you only knew in these days of trial and heartbreak – heartbreak out, he had never cared that much – in these days of trial how much you have come to mean to me. All very chaste and proper, she was still wasting: nothing but a willing shoulder in the twilight for his weary head—

Until at last – fairly soon, why spin it out when we had so many other things to get on with? – the essential was accomplished and she breathed her last. He held one hand and I the other. A final anguished flutter of her eyelids, a final anguished whisper take care of him for me Sarah in the difficult years ahead, and all was over.

Difficult years ahead was what she thought, I had other plans, but still it was a lovely scene with a funeral to follow even lovelier. White roses from Moose Jaw, mountains of white roses a whole freight car piled to the top with them, wreaths and sprays and Gates Ajar, and while the choir sang *Safe in the Arms of Jesus* – surely that was fair – I sat beside him in the mourners' pew and discreetly held his hand . . . . Six months, we owed it to her memory, and then—

The things I knew, fat-assed gawky little girl with pigtails riding Jake to Happy Haven country school, years and years before movies, at least before I saw one, and all about veils and orange blossoms and five-tiered wedding cakes, poor Mother and her stories if she could have guessed the primrose paths of homicide and lust, oh yes, she had orange blossoms – in Owen Sound, sixty years ago, I can just see them – and a cake with almond icing an inch thick, that's right an inch, you never saw such a cake it stood this high, enough for two hundred – what are almonds, well if you've never tasted them it's rather hard – no, not at all like peanuts – well, maybe roughly, the same size – oh yes, all the best cakes—

Piling it on, holding her own against the pork barrel and the five-dollar coat from Eaton's. . . . She had had more, a little more. There had been a seven-roomed house with a red carpet and white lace curtains in the parlour, beautiful curtains, oh yes so long they spread away out over the carpet half-way to the middle of the room – then what about your feet well naturally you watched where you put your feet. There had also been a lawn with lilacs and a pine tree – but you must remember, an enormous pine, sometimes I used to take you over to visit your grandmother and she'd spread a blanket for you to sit under it with your dolls. A horse, of course they had had a horse, cutter for winter and buggy for summer, a red cutter just like Dr. Hunter's and their buggy too had had yellow wheels. Sundays when the weather was good they all went to church carrying lovely blue and yellow parasols – no of course people didn't laugh, such a thing to say—

A hardware store in some little town near Owen Sound, pots and buckets, nails and screws, was that so grand that she could talk down to poor Father? All right, your father had a hardware store and my father's father, what did he have? Well, your father's father had a little property and your father was a bit wild – now just what did that mean and why couldn't she explain? Cards, drink – the reason perhaps they came West to Happy Haven? Whatever it was she took it out of him. He smoked, that was the only thing. He had a pipe and the tobacco came in little red and yellow bags with a string, Old Chum it was called and we could get it at the store for butter and eggs just like groceries – he always gave the bags to me – and that was the one thing she didn't seem to mind. Sometimes she'd say the pipe's never out of your mouth and the way I've got to skimp and save and bleach flour bags but still they seemed to have agreed, that is to say she had agreed, that he had a right to it.

The only time he ever stood up to her at least the only time I ever heard him and at that he didn't really stand up to her she went right ahead anyway but at least he said for Christ's sake Ida don't be such a damned fool, that time was the trees.

For they had had trees too in Owen Sound, not just the pine that I was supposed to have sat under but maples and elms, poplars and balm of Gileads, wonderful trees big and shady the streets all lined with them and not a reason in the world we couldn't have trees in Happy Haven too, people out here were so shiftless that was all.

Well what about the trees we do have, the willows and poplars in the coulee on the way to school some of them a good ten feet, all the saskatoon and chokecherry bushes and the little grey wolf willows in the pasture – but oh no, Sarah, those aren't trees, not real trees, those are just scrub and that was why, so far away from trees, from real trees, her own daughter not even knowing what a real tree looked like, she decided she would plant her own.

A hundred from Brandon – I think it was Brandon, there was a special farm, a nursery – terrible wormy-looking little things when they came three or four inches all paper and mud, a grove, she said, on the north side of the house it will be a windbreak it will stop the blizzards and keep the snow away. The day they came poor Father I'll never forget the way she had him on the run, running herself and yelling get them lined up straight and not so close they're going to grow the branches are going to spread you should leave at least ten feet, four rows of twenty-five each, the grove, beautiful Manitoba maples; and then all summer water water as if there wasn't already enough to do, come on now Sarah another couple of pails won't hurt you, petting and fussing counting every leaf and still they died not all but more than half, even with bits of shingle stuck in the ground at a slant to shield them from the wind and sun oh yes, we did that too; and then four or five months later wrapping the ones that were left in bits of old sack and sweaters to help them through the winter, that was when Father said for Christ's sake Ida don't be such a damned fool, not that it bothered her she was going to have her grove she was going to show Saskatchewan.

In the spring she wanted to order more to bring her hundred up to strength, it would have taken at least seventy-five, and that day there was another row, one of the best, they swore at each other – the words she knew – you have your damned Old Chum the pipe's never out of your mouth that was one of the times she said it but still he wouldn't, he did stand up to her, sending more money absolutely no, so it ended up she had only twenty or twenty-five, pretty scrubby-looking too and not exactly blizzard-stoppers, but still they stayed alive and showed it could be done, all you needed was a little drive and enterprise and a daughter who could pour.

In the meantime there were the caraganas up a good three feet – she'd planted them when they first came west, you only need seeds – but they of course weren't real trees either, just a hedge to keep the barn away. That was the idea when she put them in – grunting and clucking round the door there's nothing worse – only all the hedge did was drive the pigs and chickens crazy wanting to know what was on the other side and I was the one, quick Sarah quick, a good shoo this time go right after them they've got to learn, they're going to ruin the flowerbeds.

I had a stick for the pigs and what an uproar when I fixed up a new one with a nail at the end, such thick tough skins it was the only way. Oh Sarah I'm ashamed of you that's terrible that's cruel, well for a change then do your own shooing try saying nice little piggy yourself and see how fast they run, now no more lip young lady the hips and legs on you a little exercise is just what you need and besides what about your lovely bachelor buttons and nasturtiums? *Ah-ha* and wasn't she the old smoothy though so they were *my* lovely bachelor buttons now, damned scrawny things, if she thought I was running my hips to the bone—

Still it was all part of being a Robinson who else in Happy Haven had a hedge to keep the barn away and who with a background of almond icing parasols and Manitoba maples was a better choice for the lonely Dr. Hunter, who could better hold her own among the town's best families? Not only taste but natural intelligence too, exceptionally endowed – the wedding for instance and the supper afterwards, seven tiers and raspberry vinegar, attending to it all myself while the town wondered and admired, how fortunate that this time he has found the woman he deserves, presiding socially, and at the same time just look at the ardour in his eyes—

Oh yes, I knew some things and not just about parasols and almond icing either, the facts of life as well, eleven twelve and a virgin good at picking up things was right at least I knew what each side has and why, I didn't go through it all, the runaway and the wasting, just to sit with him in the twilight holding hands.

There were the chickens of course with the roosters chasing them and Mother saying Sarah don't look you ought to be ashamed, enough to make you catch on, the same when the stallion came the poor shaggy little horse pulling the two-wheeled cart with the half-breed driving at least she said he was a half-breed it made him that much worse, he looked black all right although I never got close enough to see, just from the window, who but a half-breed anyway would do such a disgusting job, always hunched over elbows on knees and the big black stallion prancing behind, neighing and snorting, such a fuss making sure everybody knew, a few times I even saw him showing off just a very brief glimpse though, you stay right here young lady you can peel the potatoes and keep away from that window it's time you were doing more to help me anyway never mind why, you stay right here. Poor woman the straight no-nonsense head on her too, did she really think or was it just in case, so she could say with a clear conscience for all Happy Haven to hear well Heaven knows I did my best to keep her innocent.

At school the same, warnings warnings, funny for someone from a good place like Owen Sound how much she knew about what went on in Happy Haven. The stable was the place, the loft, those of us who lived three or four miles away and had to drive or ride, I rode Jake, we all brought oats anyway, never hay, so there was no need of a loft but somebody had had the idea and when the weather wasn't good up they'd go, and when it was there was a little dip behind the school, willows and a creekbed, but nearly half a mile so they had to make it fast and eat their lunch on the way. Sometimes they would come back a few minutes late, oh they'd been picking flowers or catching gophers, and next day have to stay in at recess to make up for lost time oh yes, things went on all right, real things, they really did it, never me though because I was one of the good girls.

Watch it now if they start talking dirty or trying to play you slap them hard and yell. You don't know what I mean? Well, you will if they start, remember now no touching, they're just like animals it's the way they've been brought up, run for all you're worth and tell the teacher it's what she's there for.

Lona Painter was the worst or maybe the best depending on how you looked at it. There were others who did sometimes too but she was the steadiest, the boys took turns, at least the ones she liked. On my side there was a girl called Fern with big teeth and frizzy hair more like a Russian thistle I used to think than a fern and another called Beulah with glasses always pulling her mouth in trying to look intelligent, another too I can't remember, we were the good ones we would sit on the steps at noon talking about our lessons and new underwear as good girls should, telling nice stories and calling each other liars while the others were up in the loft or down among the willows it was terrible—

But still Lona was my friend. Instead of turning up her nose at me for being so good she always talked and took an interest, very sympathetic, in winter she'd wrap me up before I started home, scarf around my face and mitts on properly to make sure nothing would freeze – Jake was so high I got all the wind – and besides, the most important thing, she'd help me up.

A very big horse with a mean wall eye but safe, and three and a half miles he was the only way. If someone didn't help me – short and fat, it was starting even then – I had to do it from the manger inside the stable or climb up on a fence post, books, lunch pail, reins, and if I dropped anything then I had to get off and start all over. The manger was bad because he'd jump and skitter, always in such a hurry to start home, and so big going through the door it was low he'd make me bump my head, but the fence was worse except I didn't bump my head, because instead of standing lined up quiet and close beside it he'd swing his hind end straight out as far as he could from the post I'd climbed up on, ears back, wall eye rolling, and sometimes it would take ten or fifteen minutes tugging and swearing you wall-eyed old bastard just wait till I get you home before he'd give in and let me on.

The boys oh yes the boys, they were always ready to help but the idea was to feel my leg while they were doing it, one of the good girls they thought it would be fun and besides might bring me round. Always trying to get their hands inside my bloomers – navy blue, heavy material, because riding Jake my skirts naturally came up and red or white flannel drawers showing would have been a disgrace but nobody could say anything about bloomers, perfectly decent – and in that position trying to get up on Jake and my hands full it was hard to stop them. Sometimes they'd get their fingers an inch or two under the elastic and I knew that that was the beginning, a little farther I'd turn black.

That was what she always warned, let the boys get close and start doing things before you're fifteen you'll get covered with pimples and then turn black, there was a girl in Owen Sound a terrible sight she always had to wear a veil and what happens after fifteen well by that time you've got more sense and if you haven't you deserve everything you get. A confusing answer – so with fear of turning black and having to wear a veil and so much trouble getting up on Jake I was naturally always glad of Lona's helping hand.

Wondering all the time though why doesn't she turn black. Once she had some pimples on her chin, little ones, a rash, and I used to look every morning to see how they were coming along – now she'll be sorry, this must be it for sure, I wonder how she'll look with a veil – but instead of spreading and turning black they just cleared up like ordinary pimples, too many eggs her mother said, and Lona kept right on disappearing up the loft or down to the creekbed, by the looks of things having the time of her life.

Friendlier and friendlier, knowing I shouldn't but still, until the day she said why don't you and Jake come over Saturday for a visit and I said all right, I'll ask – a very nice visit too, we had jelly, and wandering around looking her place over, calves and chickens, her father had given her a colt, I confessed I didn't know anything at all I didn't even have a little brother and when the stallion came my mother made me peel potatoes. She didn't laugh, though, very understanding, one of her aunts was like that, and it turned out she had been afraid of me all along thinking I was naturally good like Fern and Beulah, but since it was just a case of being scared she was friendlier than ever and said she would do everything she could to help.

The boys, for instance, it was time, and Herb Gillespie would be a good one to start off with. Yes, he was the nicest looking all right but she didn't mind, she'd see about it, and what was the difference between the stallion and Jake why doesn't he ever he's got one too sometimes it's out two feet, well it's because they cut him when he was a colt. Then what about boys oh no you don't have to worry they never cut boys, it's against the law – the things she knew!

But the best way naturally would be to find out for myself

so she'd speak to Herb first thing Monday morning, a good all round one not just looks either, leave everything to her. Scaring me nearly out of my wits, no no I didn't mean so soon, but the sooner the better, when you're still young there's nothing to worry about, it's all right till you're fifteen. That fifteen again, deeper and deeper yet certainly she hadn't turned black, a very good complexion in fact, pink and white, now don't be silly Sarah, you've got to make up your mind—

What with all my other problems, Mother and Jake and fractions, I'd nearly forgotten by Monday morning and then right in class, not at recess or lunchtime but right in class, she leaned across the aisle and poked me with her ruler, look quick, now's your chance while the teacher's writing on the blackboard, and across the next aisle just a seat or two back there he was showing me.

A special favour, she'd talked to him about me – holding it just so with a nice little smile and keeping his hands close so he could cover up quick if anyone else turned round, careful careful and so proud, just as if it was something he had caught, a bird or gopher, and now though wasn't I really scared, talk about a turmoil, scared to look and scared if I didn't it might hurt his feelings and I'd never have a chance to look again, scared Fern or Beulah might turn round and catch me looking, scared if I did look he would think I meant at noon that very day—

Funny, years later when I married him and he took me pure and undefiled as they say, not a black spot anywhere, funny all the times we did it and it was one thing at least he was good at we never talked once about the day in school when he took it out and showed me. Such a good-looking boy, he could have had his pick the same as Dunc, and I just passed. Nice eyes, everybody used to talk about my eyes, but maybe it was because there wasn't much else to talk about and they wanted to be polite. It's true of course your eyes are important, the way you look at a man, but still it's not what they're really after.

Lucky that Dunc and Stan take after him in looks, and even better we can all be thankful that Dunc's like me when it comes to taking hold and doing things. Herb in his own way was all right too God bless him, one of the best and I'd jump at the chance to do it again but he didn't amount to much, he liked to take things easy although give him his due he got us off the farm and into the store. Up at five o'clock in the morning, twelve hours a day on the harrow or drill and then the chores, that wasn't the life for him. Stan, I don't know – he's got his leg, and Dunc keeps picking on him – I just wish he wouldn't hang around so much with Benny. Sooner or later there'll be talk, maybe there is already for all I know, and it's going to make it hard for Dunc and Caroline—

Turning out to be such a fine girl, so much better than anybody expected, and there I was nearly sick dreading the way she'd be talking down to us saying ignorant Canadians and colonials. Plenty going on in her mind at that, a little flash sometimes the things I say, but sense enough to keep it to herself. Upward and mothers-in-law and all the old gossips we know where we can go. She's got Dunc and now Robbie – deep down inside she doesn't give a good goddam. At-a-girl, Caroline! The same with Herb, I knew he was lazy and a lot of other things, but the look in his eyes, wanting not just it but me, not just so he could relax and get a good night's sleep but because I was the one—

Funny though, I still can't understand, all the years so close yet never once to tease him, what a terrible thing to do actually take it out and show me, school of all places, no shame at all, pretending to be shocked – and never once about Lona, how many times, was she really so good, and you'd have thought—

But funnier still, wanting him so much even though I didn't know it right from that day in school, a dirty little girl trying to peek when the stallion came a disgrace to Owen Sound and yet never, absolutely never, not because I was naturally good as Lona for a while had feared, and not because I really believed I might turn black and have to wear a veil, but just because I didn't.

All the time of course there was Doc – busy with him, maybe that was why. Poor Herb, smiling, so proud of his little three-inch treasure, what chance did he have against the buffalo robe and all the other things? If he'd only known in fact how he helped, the ideas, and how I just enlarged them nearer to the heart's desire.

Maybe before Doc goes I ought to tell him – a laugh wouldn't do him any harm. Always a friend, someone to turn to and at the last so good to Herb, yet all the years never so much as a second glance, I might have been a heifer or a horse. Tell him too I should about the ringworms – more than forty years, I don't suppose he remembers. Of all things and of all places, and just when our affair was at its romantic peak. Some pimples, I thought – it's a place you ordinarily don't look. Itch itch, what on earth's wrong with you Sarah, sit still and stop scratching, it's not very ladylike. At last into her bedroom for her hand mirror, drawers down, bending and twisting into the right position to get the right light, and then for a minute or two straight into the abyss. So it was true, the mills of God grind slowly yet they grind exceeding small. First red, then black – it had never occurred to me it might be anywhere but the face. What's going to happen now though, what will she do to me? And so unfair, two or three inches up my bloomers nothing but fingers and all Jake's fault, day after day sitting on the steps with Fern and Beulah, hating it but good – oh Mother come quick, I think I've got something bad—

Laugh laugh, what a joke, trust you Sarah, you usually get them on the wrist or arm. Don't look so scared, you must have been playing with the calves, just stand there a minute and I'll put on some soda to help the itch. Now once and for all stop scratching, you only make them worse, and of all days not half an hour later who should pass but Doc – run out and stop him, do what I say and waving a towel herself as if the house was on fire. Oh Doctor, if you could have seen her with her pants down holding the glass and her eyes like saucers, Mother come quick I think I've got something bad, and then no nonsense down my drawers had to come again, naked before him in all my double doughnut glory – stop being so silly Sarah and bend over, Dr. Hunter's seen lots of little girls—

If he would only sit down – they keep crowding round him and he looks so tired . . . The time he helped me chase the pigs, I can still see him it seems like yesterday, a run and a jump and a whoop right over the caraganas . . .

"Two hundred dollars for a piano nearly fifty years old? You'd have to be out of your mind. I'd say fifty and not five cents more."

"It's up to the Auxiliary of course, but I didn't know it was so old. I'd no idea she'd brought it with her from down east."

"Not with her exactly. She sent for it."

"Not expecting when she came, I suppose, that a handsome young doctor would turn up so soon."

"With hopes, though, you can be sure of that. In the old days a lot of them came west with a man on their mind. Benny's mother was another."

"Makes you think, doesn't it, that Upward's just not the place."

"And poor big Bertha Dean – Miss Hickey when she came. She taught me a couple of years – the feet on her and the jaw. Always a sweater curling up around her hips, a blue one and a brown one—"

"I was just seven or eight. I still remember the time I had trying to find out. Mother thought I was too young."

"The mystery, of course, was how Cliff ever got started with her in the first place. Such a boy around town – and then to end the way it did."

"I can still hear my mother. Just what she could stuff into a couple of suitcases – isn't that right? The day after the funeral —"

"And nobody ever heard another word – for the children's sake, I suppose, to give them a chance to forget. Two lovely little girls, blue-eyed dolls, and Cliff was so proud of them. They were the ones who found him. A shotgun – you can imagine. He'd fixed it up some way with a piece of string tied to the trigger."

"What a lot of stories Doc could tell. I've heard he was in on it too."

"Figure it out for yourself. The girl was supposed to have been three or four months gone, she'd told somebody, and there were no further developments. She spent a few days with Maisie Bell right after the funeral, it leaked out afterwards."

"You wonder why he couldn't have taken her to Doc in the first place. Never mind him but the two little girls."

"Oh no, a decent doctor doesn't do things like that. He could have lost his practice and gone to jail."

"But since he did it anyway—"

"He did it after Cliff did it. There's a difference. A child on the way that's probably going to learn some day it was on his account his father shot himself – still legally wrong, but wouldn't you yourself be inclined to go along?"

"It's a pity he didn't do it for Benny's mother too. Better than going through with it and then doing away with herself. And poor Benny – the way he's turned out he wouldn't have been much of a loss either."

"Of course it might have just been an overdose. Nobody knows for sure. She used to get terribly worked up."

"They say the people next door used to hear her yelling at Sam she couldn't stand any more and was going to cut her throat. What an awful life for Benny. I suppose we shouldn't judge."

"And Doc's wife, poor Edith, what an awful life for her while he ran around with Maisie Bell. In public, throwing her in everybody's face."

"Three of them. When a new teacher comes to Upward she ought to be given a printed card warning her of the odds. Look at our fine-feathered Miss Carmichael over there right now with her curls and make-up. New doctor coming to town. Don't tell me she's not prowling."

"By rights she oughtn't to be here anyway. This is Doc's party – she doesn't know him. She came only last September and as far as I know she's never missed a day at school, so she can't be his patient."

"A party for the old doctor – can you think of a better place to ask questions and find out about the new one?"

"It's not just the make-up, you know. She's padded too."

"Yes, I think probably you're right . . . . Well, I can only say our little Upward certainly isn't what it used to be."

"Things move so fast these days. You wonder where it's all going to end. And the example she's setting for our girls."

"Even ten years ago anybody with that green stuff round her eyes would have been taken for a streetwalker. She'd certainly never have dared stand up in class."

"And there was poor Bertha, flat as a pancake and a face like a horse, walking off with the best catch in town."

"Blowing out his brains with a shotgun – you call that a catch?"

"I mean at the time – he could have had his pick and he picked her."

"I wonder does Miss Carmichael know about Big Anna and the handkerchief? Maybe somebody should have a little chat."

Be with me, O Lord, and help me not to despise them. Teach me humility that I may forbear from judgement, and give me the courage to look into the dark places of my own heart. Strengthen me when I falter. Shine upon me and sustain my faith. Through the dark night of doubt hold Thou my hand.

For I do falter – not in loyalty to Thee, but to the task Thou hast imposed. Why, O Lord, to what end? If they were sinners or heathen I could pray for them, labour that they might see the light, but they are already in the fold, they pay to keep it in repair, they are more secure than I. They sing *Praise God from Whom all blessings flow* with the assurance of the chosen, and there is not one word they understand. They bow their heads for the benediction, but their hearts are closed and dry.

Look at them now, how they chatter and preen. How up-to-date we are with our new hospital, even better than Comet. We'll be able to take out gallstones, we've got a machine to tell you all about your heart. But what does it profit a man that he gain a few more years if he hasn't an hour for communion with his soul?

Not a prayer, not a word of dedication. They look at us as if we were intruders. Go back to your pulpit and your mouldy little house, this isn't where you belong. We're modern here, we're with the times. Poor Joyce, her gallant little stand against the gin – well, at least she needn't know, it's one little deception I and my conscience can come to terms with . . . .So clever, such wit and daring to talk to the preacher about reproductive energy and our long Saskatchewan nights. This time tomorrow it will be all over town – Oh yes, indeed she did, and if you could have seen their faces!

And yet they want their church. They haven't the courage to say no, to speak up and say it's just a waste of time and money. They want to be married in it, their children baptized. They want the preacher when it's time to die, but the faces on them when it's time to pay. The hymnbooks are falling apart. After every service there are pages all over the floor – it sometimes takes Joyce more than half an hour to fit them back where they belong; we need a new organ, my salary's what it was five years ago; but suppers and sales, well, there's a saturation point, they can't have them for hospital and church both, and the hospital of course is an urgent need.

The same all through the war: parcels for Overseas, ciga-rettes and chocolates for the boys. Bustling and honking with importance, our parcels are bigger than Comet's, last month we knit fifty pairs of socks, but how much compassion or love did they send along, how many prayers for a kingdom of peace and goodwill? Their famous Hospital Dance – Benny Fox and his band such wonderful fellows now, they're going to do it annu-ally, a worthy cause so you must buy tickets whether or not you intend to go; three hundred and eighteen dollars, the entire proceeds, a gift. But couldn't they just occasionally – would it hurt so much – send us a cheque for twenty-five?

I know, O Lord, I know – it's so petty and contemptible. A man of God, my thoughts on higher things, on Thee, I shouldn't mind, shouldn't even see. If I could only believe that despite it all I serve, that some day the seeds will spring and bloom, but I flutter on the margin of their lives, like a leaf that has died and not yet fallen. They need me only to serve their vanity, someone to point to and say, see what fine people we are, we pay a preacher and support a church, our children go to Sunday School.

And yet I must believe, I must go on. It was I who chose and no one ever said it would be easy. I must, I must – be with me still, turn not Thy face away. For it's late – not far off fifty-five – to start out on the road selling sewing machines or encyclopaedias. And to preach and pray by rote – it was not for that I rose and followed Thee. A mealy-mouthed old sham with a bread-and-butter smile – not that, O Lord, not that!"

"Fair's fair, he'd always come. Even away back before there were cars, no matter what kind of weather or what shape the roads were in, as soon as he got the message he'd be on his way. He'd come and he'd do his best, but he was hard. It's a good many years now but I'll never forget. He took our last two calves."

"Well, I suppose he thought—"

"Yes, I suppose so too. You pay for your sugar and flour and binder twine, why shouldn't you pay your doctor bills. He had to pay his bills, he didn't enjoy driving ten or fifteen miles when it was twenty below – I know all that – but he wouldn't listen when we promised. Next year, he said, I'm fed up hearing about next year. And he took our calves."

"I know, I've heard the stories too. My sister Alice – but she says a lot of the farmers liked it that way, it was to make things easier for them. If you haven't got the cash, a calf or a steer will be just as good for me."

"That's the way he likes to tell it, but the truth is he's always been in there grabbing fast. A few times I suppose he was up against a deadbeat. Then he decided we were all deadbeats."

"I can't talk, we've never had much need of him – just plain lucky. Alice though, swears by him. I don't suppose you know but a long time ago they had a little boy – wasn't born right –

and he let the bills run on for years. Cleared up finally I think with a couple of cows, but it suited them that way. As you say, fair's fair."

"And I don't for a minute doubt that my own father was one of the deadbeats that soured him, but you see he took those two calves and one of them was mine. Nigger – six months old – I'd raised him. And something like that's awfully hard for a youngster to forget or forgive. Nine or ten. And even if I'd known he needed the money for the mortgage on his house or his wife's fur coats, I don't suppose it would have made it any easier."

"What started him I suppose was people in the old days wanting to pay with butter and eggs. Instead of spinning it out a couple of pounds a week why not just give me a calf and call it quits – easier than keeping track."

"But it's the sort of thing you don't expect of a doctor. Rounding up calves, feeling for a fat one – it takes something away. How can you look up to him?"

"You admit, though, he'd always come—"

"A lot go round saying good old Doc, forty-five years of sacrifice and service, what would we have done without him? Sounds fine, a real hero, but get down to brass tacks and he was just doing a job and taking good care he got paid for it. A good living and he knew it. Don't tell me he hung on in Upward forty-five years just because he loves us. Calves, that's what he's always been after – my Nigger."

"A battered old Ford, the same house he built over forty years ago – maybe he's been salting it away but what for?"

"I'll hand it to him the calves and steers were a smart idea. In fact I'd say he missed his calling. Shrewd – what's in it for me? They say he got the land for a song, hilly, not much good for breaking; all he had to do was fence it and put up a windmill. No time at all he had a nice little herd – his 'collections' and the increase. One of the neighbours to keep an eye on things, maybe drop round himself once a month or so. Nothing to do but call in a buyer twice a year and cash his cheques."

"It seems to work for groceries too. Look at Dunc Gillespie – two or three sections with a full-time man looking after things – and the last few years the price of beef."

"No, Dunc doesn't stand for deadbeats either – a good friend of Doc so maybe he learned from him. Groceries, though, are different. Somehow you don't mind."

"All depends on the way you look at it. A nice little house he's built for his wife."

"And by the looks of things he's getting better interest on his investment. I don't think he's had to find himself a Maisie Bell yet, and certainly Caroline's got a contented look."

"Maybe not for long, though. There's some I could name just lying low, waiting their chance. Very charming, lovely smile, but just the same she lets you know. Some of them are starting to say *Her Ladyship*."

"You're such a flatterer, Caroline, such nice compliments you pay us. Still practically a newcomer in Upward, thousands of miles from home, and always looking so happy – no other place you'd rather be."

"At the moment, yes. But just watch the corners of my mouth go down if Duncan runs off with another woman. The glummest face in Canada."

"Not much danger. He looks pretty pleased with himself too. And a good colour. You must be feeding him well."

"Well, I've learned to fry bacon and eggs the way he likes them. That starts him off and he can always nibble things in the store. Every so often his mother sends over a pie. One way and another we get along."

"Caroline, this is terribly nervy of us but we're curious – just how did you and Dunc ever get to know each other? Some of the boys when they came back had stories about picking up girls in the pubs, but nobody's going to believe that about you. Just stop in the street and look at each other? You know, lightning?"

"Well, not exactly. Not the street—"

"I'm sorry – yes, we really do have our nerve."

"No, no. I love telling how we met. I was just lost for a moment remembering . . . Not the street but fairly close – a theatre."

"You mean you were an actress? I never heard that."

"Heavens no, nothing so glamorous. It began in fact with a chocolate bar – two chocolate bars –"

"*Before* you met?"

"Well, I was with my brother Eric. He was on leave and he had a spare ticket. His lady friend had stood him up – is that how you say it? – so he condescended to take me. At intermission the burning question was chocolate: to buy or not to buy. During the war, you see, everything was strictly rationed, including chocolate. Even in the theatres: the girls would come round selling it, but you had to hand over a coupon. Well, both Eric and I had been dipping into our rations rather heavily and now we were trying to decide should we indulge ourselves and then go short for a few days, or practise restraint and spread our pleasures – the theatre tonight, a bit of chocolate the day after tomorrow. And then, right in the middle of our discussion, this big Canadian voice beside me speaks up, 'Don't use your coupons, Miss, we've got some bars to spare.'

"And there they were in the palm of his hand – two of them, and so festive-looking, silver and scarlet wrappings. Our wartime chocolate was dark and bitter and the paper always had such a waxy look. Well, while I was staring – nothing like this had ever happened to me in all my life – the big voice went on to explain they were allowed to buy two a day in their canteens and besides they were always getting them from home in parcels. He won't admit it but I think they used to carry them as bait, you know: see what I've got, Baby, come along and I'll show you more. Eric came close to spoiling things. He wasn't going to sit quietly by while his sister was accosted by a strange soldier, one of those terrible Canadians, so I had to be fairly sharp with him – don't be ridiculous, they've got nuts in them. And then to help things along the other soldier, the one with Duncan, leaned over with two more for Eric. 'Don't be shy – we've got lots.' Nuts too, so we were both lost."

"And things I suppose just carried on. Now isn't that a story!"

"Why don't you get Nellie to write it up for the *Chronicle*?"

"Well, I had a little apartment, and as Eric was staying with me right then and London was dark and terribly crowded, we all four very respectably went back for a cup of tea and Spam and beetroot sandwiches – wartime fare. We couldn't even offer them a proper drink; Scotch was under the counter at that time so it had to be a very short one. And as you say, things just carried on."

"And the other one, Saskatchewan too?"

"No, a Maritimer, and I've always felt a little guilty about him. He was such a nice boy and we just failed to keep in touch. He and Duncan didn't even know each other, they just happened to have seats together. The clubs and canteens always had a number of tickets for service men on leave and they had drawn the same theatre. Eric did his best, snapshots, jokes, dog stories, but the poor boy deserved something so much better. For the life of me, I can't even remember what he looked like."

"And during the dog stories, what about you and Dunc?"

"Well, I'm not sure about Duncan, but I was trying to remember the map of North America and fit in Saskatchewan. I'm afraid I had it at a terrible tilt, north of Manitoba and running into Hudson's Bay, and I was also wondering how bad a time I would have with Father."

"Right away then? It *was* lightning."

"At least a premonitory tingle."

"And no regrets?"

"No, I often find myself trying to remember what life was like before, what I did, what I thought about. I belong here now. Upward's my town. I'm even becoming what you call a booster."

"I don't suppose we need tell you that when you first came a lot of people were watching."

"Yes, I knew, and for a while I did tread rather warily – traveller in a foreign land – but now, even though I sometimes feel they're still watching, I'm daring to stand up and criticize, take sides. I criticize because I want it to be a better town. It's where Robbie's going to grow up, go to school, have his tonsils out, so it had better be."

"You don't miss England?"

"Little things sometimes – just today in fact, because it's

April, and I used to love walking with the dogs – but it never lasts."

"Of course we all saw the snaps Dunc sent – the whole town saw them, to say nothing of the country. Sarah used to keep them in the store – and the garden looked just like a garden in a movie. There was one you could see a side of the house with the ivy, and the roses."

"You'll maybe find this hard to believe, Caroline, but I've never seen a rose in a garden – just the ones you order for a funeral."

"Yes, the ivy is at least a hundred years old, but there's something to be said too for growing geraniums and begonias in pots. At least for me – you see I used to take the ivy and the roses for granted. Now I have my own ivy, in a pot too, growing like mad. Duncan made me a little trellis, and I'm certainly not taking it for granted. I watch every leaf as if my life depended on it. And my caragana hedge – at least eight inches high. It seems to have stood the winter."

"No plans to go back then? For a visit?"

"There's tremendous interest in Robbie, naturally – every letter the pressure mounts, snaps just won't do – so we'll probably try to arrange something within the year."

"Dunc too?"

"Well, apart from the money, it's hard for him to get away. I would really much rather have them visit us – let them see with their own eyes how their daughter's faring."

"You mean they're worried?"

"Not really, but Mother's letters always sound as if I were lost somewhere out in the wilderness, living on bark and berries. I would love to bring her as a guest to one of the Ladies' Aid meetings and watch her stuff herself. And Father, we might take him to the farm, put him on a horse and give him one of Stanley's sombreros . . . .There's Stanley now and I'm afraid he has some music with him. I think perhaps I should be with Duncan."

"Oh Dan, I thought you'd never get here. I've just had an idea."

"Well, there's nothing unusual about that, Nellie. I just hope that this time you've broken with precedent and come up with a good one."

"It's Doc – he's leaving."

"Yes dear, I know. That's why we're all here tonight."

"Don't take that tone with me. I mean there's so little time left. You should try and get something more out of him."

"More? We've known each other twenty-seven years and it seems to me his life has always been fairly open."

"But that's just it, you don't know. I overheard a bit of conversation a few minutes ago, the old story about Cliff Dean. They were talking about the baby that was on its way and never got here. He's likely done all sorts of things like that, played a part in countless little dramas."

"I'm ashamed of you, Nellie. Supposing he does come clean about a few illegal operations? What do we do? Play them up *now* in the *Chronicle*, to speed him on his way – a final burst of applause?"

"Get him talking about the old days when he first came, and you don't know what may come out. They say so many women went out of their minds and I suppose there were fights and things – poker, booze. Look at old Harry Hubbs over there – decadence with one foot in the grave if ever I saw it – and you know what you've told me about him. Well, now that Doc's leaving he may be more inclined to open up and tell things. Professional secrets – you never know."

"And say we do learn a secret or two? A hired man maybe, murdered and buried under a manure pile—"

"I just mean it would be nice if we had something more on file. After all, he's seventy-five and looking rather shaky. Well, if something happens you'll have to write another piece about him – now won't you? even if he isn't here. And you don't want just to repeat what you've been saying this time."

"Nellie, you're a goddamned ghoul."

"Never mind, you've always said that a newspaperman can't afford to be sentimental. And it's only a suggestion – at least you might draw out an anecdote or two, something to reveal the warmth and humanity of the man. All secrets, you know, aren't shameful."

"I'd say he's good for another ten years. Especially now that he'll be able to relax and take life easy."

"But that's just it, nothing to do, nothing to live for – it may be very soon."

"I don't like the way you say that – like making a doll and sticking pins in."

"He's seventy-five, Dan, we don't need pins. Do as I say and have a chat. You know – when you look back, Doc, over your forty-five years in Upward, I suppose there are certain moments that stand out. A willing ear and he'll go on forever."

"And something he's kept to himself for thirty or forty years – you think it's going to unlock his lips just asking about the moments that stand out?"

"There's such a thing as subtlety. I'm only suggesting an approach."

"Anyway, he's busy talking and they keep arriving. Right now I think I'll have a little chat with old Harry. All by himself over there in the corner, looking pretty neglected and forlorn – maybe he'd like a willing ear too."

"A beautiful little hospital just when you're ready to go. They're not even very tactful about it – of all places to hold a farewell party. Talk about rubbing in the salt!"

"Hospitals cost a lot of money, Miss Carmichael. Upward's come along about as fast as you could expect. It's had its problems."

"That's very generous of you, but still I think they could have had it twenty years ago. Look at Comet, not much bigger – and I hear that now they're planning a new wing for theirs."

"The depression spoiled a lot of plans. Remember the dust storms and the Bennett Buggies? Or maybe you weren't out west in those days. And then the war. They finally got the new school finished just when the depression hit. The old one was two rooms, then they fitted out two more – the beginners at the back of the Town Hall and the ones ready for High School over the hardware store. A town this size has to wait."

"I've just been through, operating room, delivery room, X-rays – and you've had nothing but your little black bag."

"In some ways, of course, that made it easy. After all, there's only so much you can do in your office – lance boils, set bones, say less bread and more vegetables. If it looks bad, recommend a trip to Regina or at least Comet. So in a way it will be harder for Nick. When I sent somebody to Regina and he didn't make it it was Regina's fault, not mine; but now Nick will be the one. There's nothing surer than that some of them will look wise and say we were better off with old Doc Hunter."

"This new man who's on his way – Nick, you call him – from what I hear, you think very highly of him?"

"It's a long time since I've seen him, but the reports are good. The makings of a first-rate surgeon. Nothing to worry about. Upward's going to be in good hands."

"Excuse me, Dr. Hunter, I couldn't help overhearing that remark. What makes you so sure we'll be in good hands?"

"Well, it's not just that I'm sure, Mrs. Harp, the Board's been making a few inquiries too. After all it's their concern a lot more than it is mine. Recommended all along the way; has a fine war record—"

"Well, if he's so good what's he coming to a place like Upward for? What's he coming *back* for?"

"I suppose because he's been asked back – that's one good reason. And now with the hospital Upward has a lot to offer."

"Away out here at the end of nowhere? And him with such a wonderful record?"

"No, Upward's not a bad place at all for a young doctor. He'll see a lot and he'll learn a lot. Heart cases, cancer cases, ulcers, accidents – they'll all come to him. Not like in a big city hospital where the patients are divided up among the specialists. He'll be on his own. He'll have to do his best."

"Just what we were saying, a fine chance to experiment. If his knife slips or he takes out the wrong piece that'll be fine with him – it's only Upward. Coming back to show us who's top dog now."

"If a doctor's worth his salt, Mrs. Harp, he's always experimenting – always learning – for the simple reason that no two cases are ever exactly the same. Something the patients should thank their stars for. What he learns treating one may help him to do a better job on the next. All doctors makes mistakes, the best of them; it won't be surprising if Nick makes a few too. But talking as if he was planning to cut people up to see what's going on, that's just plain ridiculous – childish. You ought to be ashamed of yourself. Upward's lucky to get him. You'll be lucky if you keep him four or five years."

"Well, I'm not ashamed of myself and we'll see to it he stays a lot less than four or five years. This is not a hunky town, Dr. Hunter. *You* don't mind the people you have for friends – you've made that plain over the years – but some of us in Upward are a little more particular. We have a hospital now that's a credit to the town and we want a doctor who's a credit to the hospital. Not Big Anna's boy."

"It's all right, Miss Carmichael, she has a right to speak her piece. There she goes, dragging off poor Ernie with her. . . . You won't believe this, but they're afraid of Nick, both of them. They haven't forgotten certain things and they think he won't have forgotten either. That's right – they think he's coming back to get even."

"All this just because he was Big Anna's boy?"

"Big Anna, his clothes, the things they ate, the garlic. The boys used to pick on him and Ernie Harp was about the meanest. The others grew up a bit, got more sense; he wanted to keep on having his fun. You know how it is – most boys clap and play with a dog, but there's always one little so-and-so who wants to kick it."

"And Nick – he just submitted?"

"Indeed he didn't, he was the toughest of them all, but they used to jump him, three or four at a time. No shame. Until the day Dunc Gillespie stepped in. He licked the blazes out of his brother Stan, and then made the others stand back while Nick licked the blazes out of Ernie. Fine, but Hallowe'en came along a day or two later and Ernie smeared Nick's windows. They had a little shoe and harness shop on Main Street. Maybe you can guess what he smeared them with."

"And Nick of course wasn't standing for that?"

"Damned near killed him. Next morning he lay in wait just outside the school grounds. Talk about black eyes and cut lips. He apparently got him by the nape of the neck and rammed his face into a fence post. I had to put in nine or ten stitches. Mrs. Harp of course went into hysterics – that's what mothers are for – and raised a terrific row with the School Board. It was nip and tuck for a few days – they wanted to expel Nick – so I took it on myself to step in. Got up at a parents' meeting they called and told them Ernie hadn't got half what was coming to him and that instead of running to the Board Mrs. Harp ought to teach her son some elementary manners."

"And saved the day—"

"Well, at least they didn't expel Nick, just a warning. That was when I went into a huddle with him and explained that sometimes you win by losing. He was a bright boy and the important thing was to get all the schooling he could and then tell the Harps and their kind where to go."

"And it's still rankling, after twenty years—"

"Give Mrs. Harp her due, she saw the light. Had a sore throat one day – sent for me, just an excuse, and we got along fine. Yes, Ernie'd been wrong but he was really such a good boy at heart and it was the others who egged him on. Anyway, there you have it. Ernie remembers – not only that time, but dozens of others – and he's scared, and his wife's scared with him. Scared Nick's coming back to take it out on them. They think all these years he's had nothing to do but remember too."

"Maybe a bit of jealousy along with it?"

"Yes, I suspect there is. Ernie's still got his little delivery truck."

"Well, this Nick certainly sounds interesting. I hope I have a chance to meet him."

"Still got your appendix?"

"A penny for them, Harry – and I'm ready to bet a lot more they're about the old days and Doc Hunter."

"Craziest thing I ever heard of, walking out just when the hospital's ready. Now he'd have a chance to show what he can do. The other day I heard somebody say all he's ever been good for is telling you to take aspirin and keep your bowels open. Made me so jumping mad if I'd been ten years younger I'd have opened his bowels for him."

"Well, Doc's never been the man to worry about what other people say. He's done a good job in Upward and he knows it. And after all, he's seventy-five, he's earned a rest."

"Doesn't mean a thing. I'm seventy-seven and I've still got all my teeth."

"You've known him a long time, Harry?"

"Nobody round here any longer. Two years ahead of him – a homestead out Happy Haven way in 1901."

"And you got to know him right after he came?"

"Maybe a year. Had some boils on my neck that kept getting worse. I'd seen him passing on his way somewhere so I went out to catch him on the way back."

"Looked after the boils all right?"

"Came back to the shack with me so he could lance them – nice and ripe – and when he saw the way I was living he gave me real old hell. That was the way we got to know each other."

"Batching, I suppose? I've heard that in the old days it was sometimes pretty grim."

"July – heat and flies and the shack closed up all day. I just used to eat and sleep and get out again fast as I could, sort of keeping my eyes shut."

"And Doc jumped in and made you open them. He's always been good at that."

"Well, first he just sort of sniffed – you know, bad butter and blankets. Then he saw the towel."

"You did your own laundry too?"

"You mean washing? Well, I didn't used to do too bad a job in the winter because you've always got a good fire going anyway and it's easy to heat water. You don't get things so white maybe but at least they're not what you'd call real dirty. Summer, though, when it's hot and you've been out in the sun all day a big fire's the last thing – just enough to fry your pork and make a cup of tea. A few chips that'll burn up fast and then go out again."

"What about bread? Bake it yourself?"

"No, got it from a neighbour and it was terrible. Wet in the middle. She was English and she used to say I'm afraid it's a bit sad this week. It was always sad. Most of the time I'd just eat the crust – there'd be a lump in the middle of the loaf as big as your fist."

"A lump of what? The dough?"

"That's right, the sad stuff. Sometimes I'd let it dry out and then sort of fry it in the pan with the pork, but still it'd be sad. There'd even be things in it – maybe a few hairs, maybe flies. Oh, she was a real high-class lady, always telling you about what she'd been used to in England. Butter the same – Mrs. Pim – a sight you'd never forget. Used to go trolloping round in her bare feet and her hair down her back."

"Nobody else? Nobody better?"

"She was the closest, just about half a mile. And another thing, she'd let me wait and pay after threshing. Not much cash in those days – always a bad stretch from about May to September."

"Sad bread and salt pork in July. It's a wonder you didn't have a lot more than boils."

"That's what Doc said, you've got to eat something green. All kinds of orders – sheets and towels – most of it in one ear and out the other. But what he did was make me look around and see things for myself, see it wasn't going to work."

"Forty-five years ago I don't suppose they had vitamin pills."

"Oh, he had pills and things. After he'd cleaned up the boils he gave me a couple and said come to town in a day or two, don't put it off, and he'd have a bottle ready for me at the drug store – something to clean the blood. Well, I just looked at him and said, sure Doc, that's what I'll do. Fellow in the drug store, dead years now, wouldn't give a homesteader five cents credit, everybody knew and I guess Doc knew too. Anyway, a few days later, maybe a week, I came in from the field and there was the bottle waiting for me. In those days you never locked your door. He'd left the bottle and a couple of clean towels and guess what else? Half a dozen tins of tomatoes."

"I suppose he thought that even with all the vitamins cooked out they'd at least perk up your appetite."

"Never tasted anything so good in my life. Didn't even have a can-opener – took the butcher knife and punched a couple of holes. Drank the juice off straight and then dumped the rest in the pan with the pork. And the clean towels – they got me started. The shack that night you could have killed a chicken and left it to cook on the table, closed up all day and the sun a scorcher, and you know what I did? I got a big fire going and heated a couple of pails of water and had a real wash all over. See what I mean? That's Doc Hunter."

"You said something a minute ago, Harry, that he made you see yourself and he also made you see it wasn't going to work. What did you mean by that?"

"The farm, the homestead – just wasn't getting anywhere. Living like a pig and no future. That's what he said – my God, man, have you no self-respect? And that was about it. What little I had left was going fast. And debts, getting in deeper and deeper. Oh, I hung on a couple of years, but right from the day he came to fix the boils it was over. He made me see things. I was on my way out."

"What was wrong? You didn't like farming?"

"No good at it – things kept breaking. And my horses – always had sore shoulders. Raw and red, sometimes so bad I didn't have the heart to work them. I was always careful too. Half a dozen times a day used to wash all round where the collar sits because it's the salt and sweat that burns, but the sores kept coming anyway. Oh, I wasn't the only one. There were lots who'd just take the whip, maybe because they had to – wife, family, what's a man to do? You need the crop, no time for being soft. I had only myself to think about."

"What made you come west to take up land in the first place?"

"A hundred and sixty acres free, chance of buying another hundred and sixty at three dollars an acre – seemed a good idea. Lots of stories about bumper crops, how the west was going to boom."

"A bit of the pioneer spirit, then, that made the west?"

"Well, the folks were all for it. Small town in Nova Scotia – worse even than Upward for talk."

"You mean they wanted to get rid of you?"

"Not *rid* of me, exactly, just out of the way. You know – families—"

"Don't tell me you were trying your hand at homebrew away back then."

"No, I started the homebrew here. Just playing round a little, nothing really bad."

"Sounds like another man's wife."

"Well, some of that, and poker. I'd got myself a name. And a couple of horse deals. I didn't exactly *have* to get out of town, but I wasn't helping things for my two sisters, both up in their twenties and starting to worry would anybody want to marry them. No future for me there anyway, so when the family raked up a thousand dollars—"

"A thousand? Some of the oldtimers have told me they landed with a hundred. Had to build their shack and buy horses and implements all on credit."

"That's right, a nice start, and I just kept going downhill. That's what I meant about seeing it wasn't going to work. Living hard for nothing, living like the Pims."

"And what did Doc think?"

"Just what I'm telling you. Not the first time when he came about the boils, but later. Get a wife, he said, or get out. Living by yourself like this you'll go off your head. And he was right, I was on the way. Used to talk to myself and write out lists of

Odd Jobs to Do – a new one every week. Then I'd make a trip to town just for the mail on the chance there'd be a letter from the folks with five or ten dollars in it; and when there was, instead of spending it sensible, I'd get a bottle and shut myself up in the shack and drink. Looking across the prairie – just couldn't take it. In those days there used to be a lot of coyotes; at night they'd sit in front of the shack not twenty-five yards away and howl, like they were waiting, and I was so far gone I caught myself a couple of times opening the door and howling back – all right, you slinky bastards, I can do it too."

"What about those *Odd Jobs*? Ever do them?"

"Oh no, that wasn't what they were for."

"Then why the list?"

"Oh no, they weren't for doing. I'd get a feeling sometimes that I had to tell somebody, write a letter, tell what it was really like, the prairie and the Pims and the horses with their sores, but there was nobody to write to, not a letter telling those things. So I'd get a piece of paper and just sit looking at it a while, sort of wondering, and then not knowing what else to write I'd make a list – like putting the mattress out to air and getting putty to fix the windows before freeze-up, all kinds of things, mending harness, fixing the stable floor – things I'd no intention of doing, couldn't do, but just writing them down sort of gave me a feeling I was still all right. Oh yes, looking back now I can see I was well along."

"And did something happen to bring things to a head?"

"Doc, always Doc. One day I was in town, in for the mail as usual, and he came up to me on the street and said you don't smoke, do you, and I said no, that's one thing, and he just stood there a minute, sort of thinking me over, and then said all right, I'll let you know. Not another word what it was all about, just walked off and then about a week later he drove past and stopped with the big news he'd found me a job. Twenty dollars a month and a place to sleep. Livery stable. Chances now and then to make extra, driving. Somebody who didn't smoke, that was important. Nothing much to do, just be there nights in case of fire."

"And your farm – the homestead?"

"Walked off and left it. Brought the horses in, plenty of room in the stable, and told Pim to cut the crop. Took my time selling and didn't do too bad. When I'd paid off the mortgage I ended up a couple of hundred in the clear. The horses one and two at a time another couple of hundred."

"And you liked it better? No more lists of *Odd Jobs to Do*?"

"Best time of my life. Nice little room with a bed and a stove and a table for things. Nice smell of horses and hay – good for sleeping. Just the horses and a collie called Mack."

"Then why give it up? Something happen?"

"The twentieth century – ever heard of it? What kind of future was there in a livery stable?"

"What did Doc have to say when you started branching out?"

"Branching out? Well, I didn't give it up till 1917 or '18. There was a war on, maybe you heard about that too. They were recruiting all the young fellows to go and fight Kaiser Bill. Remember the posters – raping the women and sticking bayonets through the babies? So that was when I got a job in the garage, better money and keeping up with the times."

"What I meant—"

"Sure, Dan, I know what you mean – damned old snooper, worse than the women. Because I'd been to Regina a few times and brought back a friend—"

"Never in the business?"

"Just expenses – nothing in it for me. Don't suppose all told more than ten or fifteen times. Just a favour for some of the City Fathers. Everybody needs a change now and then. But no use trying to pump me. I've never told names and I'm not telling now."

"One of these days, Harry, we'll have to have a party for you too. And write you up in the *Chronicle* – one of Upward's outstanding benefactors – favours for the City Fathers, good homebrew—"

"I'll admit I made out all right with the homebrew. Just seemed to hit it right. A lot of stuff they were making was poison, burn your belly out with a couple of swigs, even turn you blind, but mine was nice and smooth. Good kick, too."

"Yes, I remember—"

"I'll say you remember. When you get round to writing me up for your paper don't forget to put yourself in as one of my customers."

"Just supposing I do sometime – the changes you've seen, fifty years of Saskatchewan history – what other favours have you done the town?"

"Run some good poker games – saved a lot of fellows from going crazy sitting home every night looking at the same old face."

"An occasional friend from Regina, good homebrew, a place to spend the evening – sure there's nothing else?"

"Don't forget I drove Doc all through the flu."

"An emergency? You got time off from the garage?"

"Sure it was an emergency – dying so fast they couldn't give them proper funerals, just the preacher to say a couple of prayers. And then he went down too."

"You were the only one available?"

"No, I don't suppose I was the only one, but Doc was used to me. I looked after his team anyway and sometimes I drove him in winter when the roads were bad."

"But the flu was 1918. He had a Ford by then."

"Still needed a team for winter. They didn't keep the roads open then like now. After a bad blizzard it'd sometimes be three or four days before a car could get through. Kept his team till about '20 or '21. Liked horses, hated giving them up. And he liked driving himself but sometimes he'd be tired, calls coming in fast, and then he'd take me."

"You didn't get the flu?"

"No, Doc didn't either, and you know why?"

"Let me guess – because every night you both drank a couple of quarts of your famous homebrew?"

"No, I wasn't making homebrew in '18, but three or four times a day we'd both take a good slug of Scotch. People were all dowsing themselves with eucalyptus – oil of eucalyptus, ever smell it? – but one day just between ourselves Doc told me that for all the good it did they might as well whiff vinegar. Except sometimes it could help if they thought it helped, know what I mean? So he'd say sure, just the thing, use plenty."

"He had you driving so he could sleep in the car, between calls – right?"

"He'd sleep while I was driving, getting him there, and I'd sleep while he was inside trying to fix them up. And there was nothing, absolutely nothing, he could do – he used to tell me. They died or got better depending on themselves, the shape they were in, but still he'd go because they called him. I remember he said one day you could do it, Harry – tell them to stay in bed and keep warm and take soup. It's crazy but they call me and I'm the doctor so I've got to go. Sometimes maybe it helps same as the eucalyptus because they think it helps, just seeing me, having me take their pulse and listen to their lungs, but if you want to know the truth not doing one goddam thing."

"Being so close to him in those days, I suppose you remember his wife."

"Sure I remember her – a real bitch."

"Maybe that's unfair. I've heard the stories too, but you know Upward—"

"I'm not talking about stories, I'm talking about her. Wouldn't even let me in the house, used to make me stand waiting on the steps – stay where you are, the Doctor won't be long. Sometimes I'd be damned near froze."

"Maybe she'd heard about your friends from Regina."

"Maybe, but what about the way she treated Doc?"

"Well, how did she treat him? Wait for him at the door with a rolling pin?"

"One thing for sure, if she'd treated him right he wouldn't have played around with Maisie. What do you think he married her for, listen to her thump the piano? Sometimes you could hear it right across town. Maisie's another you should be writing up for the *Chronicle* – lots of good things about her, but she wasn't what he wanted. He just made do with her because he wasn't getting what he had a right to get at home."

"Of course, Harry, you don't know—"

"Sure I know. I don't go round saying it – now's the first time because you've got me started – but I know."

"You mean Doc told you?"

"Doc tell things like that about his wife? Oh no, not even to me."

"And yet you know."

"Away back, Dan, not just once but plenty of times, he's brought the team around to the stable after a call, and instead of just handing them over to me he'd come in. Or maybe if I was driving he'd say don't drop me off at the house, I'll come round to the stable with you. And we'd have a drink, maybe play poker a while. Didn't want to go home, hated it, and no place else to go. He'd let her think he was still away on a call. And at that it didn't always work. Somebody'd see him driving into town and tell her – then she'd think he was over again with Maisie. Don't talk about stories to me. I'm talking about what I watched."

"And you think maybe there wasn't so much between him and Maisie?"

"That, Dan, was something I didn't watch. Sure he was in her place a lot because he had sick people staying with her. Sure she'd phone or run out on the street after him because sick people sometimes have bad turns. And after he'd fixed them up again I wouldn't be surprised if he stayed a while and played poker with her too. But I'm only saying I wouldn't be surprised. Doc could tell a joke and he liked to hear new ones, but how he made out himself, oh no, nothing like that."

"Don't worry, Harry, I'm not trying to pump you. My piece about Doc is all written and set. But you're an old friend, I suppose no one knows him better. What about the stories he was such a hard collector, when a man couldn't pay he'd take his cattle?"

"Sure he was hard – if a man owed it and had it, why not? If he thought the fellow was putting it on a bit, poor crop, sore back, wife up the stump again, that was when he'd turn tough. I've heard him – real tough. But if somebody was up against it and trying – and you didn't fool Doc easy – then he'd let it slide. I don't say he'd let it keep on sliding. He had his living to make like everybody else."

"Then you'd say tough but fair? He wouldn't take a man's last cow?"

"He bought the farm and started taking cattle, Dan, about the time people started buying cars. Remember there was a spell when things were looking up a little – about ten years – after the war a bit and before the bad times set in. Sort of went crazy, a lot of them. You'd see a little tarpaper shack out on the prairie and a car at the door damned near as big as the shack. That was when. You can buy gas for your Chevy and Studebaker, goddam you, you can help buy gas for my Ford."

"It's true he used to hire a truck sometimes? Drive out and load up what he wanted?"

"Not what he wanted, what was coming to him. A lot of times I was the one driving the truck, and just like you say, tough but fair. And only after he'd waited a couple of years – somebody trying to wriggle out. Later when he had the farm and you might say was in the business, well then he'd just as soon get paid that way. In a year sometimes they'd be worth double, and the cows would calve. A lot of times it was the way the farmer liked it too."

"Dunc Gillespie has a farm and takes cattle just the same – learned I suppose from Doc?"

"Other way round – it was Herb, Dunc's Old Man. Long before he came to town and started himself, that's what he used to say to Doc, why don't you take cattle? It's hard for a farmer sometimes to scrape up cash but he can usually spare a calf. So Doc started first but he didn't think first."

"The new man – Nick, Big Anna's boy, you must remember him – you think it was Doc who put him through?"

"Doc never talked much about him, but maybe. Used to take him with him on calls sometimes – always interested."

"This is between ourselves, of course, but I can't think how else."

"Maybe. Remember Nick's Old Man? Little John they called him – skinny little fellow with a big moustache falling down around his chin, handlebars. Always something wrong with him, not enough blood and a cough. Well, sometimes if it was just one call and not much chance of getting paid any other way, Doc would take a couple of chickens, maybe butter and eggs and a sack of potatoes, and he'd give them to Anna so she could feed him up. Not always, but a lot of times. If I was driving he'd have me take them in. Sometimes even when I wasn't he'd come round to the stable for me anyway – didn't want to be seen carrying them in himself, at least not too often. Scared, I suppose, somebody'd start another story. Anna used to work for his wife, three or four days a week, washing and cleaning."

"Did he talk much about them?"

"Once I remember when he was trying to send little John to Fort Qu'Appelle. You know, where they've got the hospital for t.b. – the place he died—"

"The sanitarium—"

"That's it. Anna didn't want him to go, scared what they'd do to him, thought she could do better herself at home, and Doc had a fight on his hands. One day he was cursing away at her all the trip, damned stupid woman, can't knock anything into her head – it's not good for them all living in that little place with a man that's got t.b., it's not good for Nick—"

"He was worried about Nick?"

"Well, I suppose t.b.'s something you don't play round with."

"Just between ourselves, did you ever wonder—"

"No, Dan, I didn't ever wonder. When it comes to that kind of wondering you can do enough for two. I can tell you though that Nick and little John weren't the only ones. He did lots of things, for lots of people."

"For instance?"

"The bad years, '33 and '34, in there – remember the way they used to ride the freights, good-for-nothing bums a lot of them, and some just up against it. No jobs, no crops. You'd see them sometimes on the boxcars sitting up on top like a lot of crows – remember? Well, there was an old man one day fell off, not so old as me now but up around sixty-five or seventy. Somebody found him lying down by the tracks. Couldn't take any more – a funny look in his eyes. I helped carry him up to Maisie's. Sure, where else? Kept him there a week, then sent him off again, like as not with some cash in his pocket. That was one. Another time there'd been a fight – a young fellow some of them had been trying to play around with. He'd fought back and got a jack-knife in his belly. Sure, Doc again – sewed him up and fed him up. Those were two I saw with my own eyes, but they weren't the only ones. Heart as big as an ox if he thought you needed it. Nick was just another."

"I think you know I've always had a very high regard for him myself—"

"Even supposing what's on your mind is true, what difference does it make now? Why snoop around to start another story?"

"No, Harry, I've already got my story. Doc himself has seen it—"

"You know what Doc once said to me? Harry, he said, if neighbours slept together more and talked about each other less, things would be a lot better all round. Now there's something for you to put in your paper."

"Nellie, I've made a decision. Do you know what I'm going to do?"

"Tell me, Dan, but don't forget your pressure. You look a little flushed."

"This week it's Doc, next week Nick, and the week after that I'm going to write up Maisie Bell."

"Wonderful, Dan, just what I've been waiting for. All the years she's been serving the town and never a word of thanks. Only do be prudent. Certain people – you know what their response will be. We must prick the town's collective conscience very gently."

"Prudence and pricks be damned, Nellie, we'll slash them to the bone. We're the Press, aren't we? We have traditions, we have principles—"

"Then I'm with you every question mark and comma of the way. I'll go around and see her tomorrow and arrange an interview. She may have some old pictures."

"We'll both interview her, different angles. A few days interval – give her time to think and come back on what she's said. Old Harry just dropped a couple of things. You remember back in the depression days when all the hungry down-and-outers were riding the freights? Well, one old man fell off, collapsed, and what do you think happened? Doc took him to Maisie's and she kept him for a week. Then there was a fight and a boy was knifed – same story, a month. Now isn't that drama for you?"

"Not just drama, Dan, *high* drama."

"And that's only scratching the surface."

"Here all these years we've been ambling along at our petty pace, immersed in our gossip and squabbles, while she has been doing big things, important things."

"We'll give Upward something to gossip and squabble about. We'll let them see the kind of paper we are. We'll show our muscle."

"Bravo, Dan, just don't forget you still haven't finished with Doc. And you haven't very long. Tonight may be your last chance."

"That's right, the obituary. See what can be captured with a willing ear."

"I have a message for you from Caroline. You're to sit down and stay sitting down. You've been on your feet again for the last half hour."

"Hello, Benny, I've been trying to talk and listen to you at the same time. I don't think anybody's put a finger on the piano in the last twenty years – not since Edith."

"The tone's fine. It just needs tuning, maybe a few new felts. The Hospital's very lucky."

"I don't think the Hospital wants it. As soon as my back's turned they'll probably try selling it. But I couldn't sell it myself. Sentimental in my old age."

"I know – there's something about a piano. I'd be sentimental too."

"I nearly gave it to you and then I thought hell, he's got his own, he'll only have to sell it too."

"I'm glad just the same you thought of me."

"Something else, Benny, there's a pile of music—"

"And you don't want to sell that either?"

"Don't suppose I could give it away, let alone sell it. *Beautiful Ohio* and *The Missouri Waltz* – remember those oldtimers? *Roses of Picardy* and *Little Grey Home in the West*. Terrible old stuff but what am I to do with it? A lot of the old war songs – *There's a Long Long Trail* and *Keep the Home Fires Burning* – a pile of it this high. I don't suppose you'd want to look it over?"

"I'll be around in the morning. How's eleven?"

"Supposing I send it over, the whole pile? Keep anything you want and throw out the rest."

"That'll be better, I can take my time. But you don't have to send it over, I'll pick it up."

"A couple of weeks now I've been looking at it – just looking, turning it over—"

"The rest of your packing done?"

"Almost – just a few things to sell or give away. Dunc and Mrs. Green are looking after them."

"And then it'll be Nick – Nick the Hunky . . . . He never had much use for me, but just the same we had a lot in common."

"He'll fit in all right. Maybe it'll take a month or two, but you'll see."

"I remember you used to take Dunc and him with you sometimes when you went to the country . . . . Once the teacher called Dunc up and had him tell the whole room how you sewed up somebody. I was a bit jealous – of them both."

"I used to take Nick and Dunc because they seemed interested. I thought they might make doctors, both of them. And even away back then I always thought of you as the boy who played the piano."

"That's right, off to take my lesson all dressed up pretty in my Sunday clothes and bow tie."

"Nothing wrong with playing the piano, Benny. I imagine you get as much out of life as most people. Don't forget Nick had his bad times too."

"We had a lot of them together. He had the big boots his father made for him and an old fur cap, and I had my bow ties and boater. Fun for everybody. What I can't understand is why he's coming back."

"Maybe to lay a few ghosts. Take a long hard look at the town and see it for what it is."

"Do you think the old days still bother him?"

"Don't they you?"

"Yes, but I'm not Nick. He was always so sure of himself, no matter what they said or did. They never made a dent. The look on his face sometimes, ready to spit on the whole pack, the whole town."

"A town you're ready to spit on, Benny, is a town you hate, and hate's no good if you want to grow. Maybe the best way to get it out of your system is to come back – see it's not worth hating."

"You told him that?"

"I said you'll learn a lot in Upward – four or five years and you'll be ready to move on to something better. And I think maybe he picked it up. Maybe not knowing he was picking it up, but picking it up just the same. He's no fool. He knows what he needs, even though he doesn't know he knows."

"And that's what you picked up, that he knows?"

"Well, he's never been one for what you might call confidences – letters always short and shy. But yes, I picked it up."

"All along you've been in touch?"

"As I say, neither of us ever wrote long letters."

"I remember when his mother died he just disappeared. Nobody knew anything. You had something to do with that?"

"He was fifteen and he'd just finished High School. The lumber yard offered him a job – working on the books a couple of hours a day and the rest of the time stacking lumber. Forty dollars a month – big money – and I said forget the lumber yard, get going and get going fast."

"Just a few minutes ago, Stan was wondering what we'll call him –Nick or Dr. Miller."

"Well, I'd at least try Nick, and see. It might help him feel that the old days are behind everybody, that Upward's his town."

"He was never scared of Upward. I don't think it ever impressed him. I was the scared one. I used to smile at everybody; see what a nice boy I am. The teacher I went to in Comet thought I should be serious about the piano – Mozart, Chopin – and I think maybe that was what I really wanted too. But who was going to listen? I'd been Mamma's boy all dressed up playing little minuets and preludes long enough. I liked it when the boys wanted something with a good beat and I could play *Yes Sir, She's My Baby*."

"Don't expect too much. Remember, he'll have made adjustments too."

"Oh no, I'm not thinking about him that way. Just curious, what he'll be like. If he'll remember me, want to remember."

"For one thing, he'll probably be busy. Doing all the work I've had to send to Comet and Regina. New hospital, up-to-date equipment – a lot of the old ladies are going to start wondering if maybe they shouldn't be looked into too."

"Doc, you're leaving and I may not have another chance to ask you: did my mother kill herself?"

"I don't know, Benny. She used to have nervous headaches, bad ones, and I used to give her something for them – a lot stronger than aspirin – and warn her never to take more than two. The bottle was empty and she'd had the prescription filled the day before, but I don't know if she took them deliberately or if it was an especially bad headache. She used to get worked up – I daresay you remember. Always after me for something stronger. She used to take brandy too."

"But it was the pills? Nothing else?"

"They were fairly strong, and apart from her nerves she was a healthy woman, so I'd say yes, it was the pills . . . . But what you're thinking is wrong. You weren't to blame."

"She always did her best to make me think I was. As far back as I can remember, long before I understood what had happened: if it hadn't been for me she wouldn't be living in a god-forgotten hole like Upward, if it hadn't been for me she wouldn't be tied up to an ignorant barber. Believe it or not, it took me years, long after she was dead, to get my head up enough to ask why it was my fault, not hers."

"She was an unhappy woman and as I say she used to get

worked up; but your fault, no, I'm sure she never really thought that. Maybe she took it out on you sometimes, the way we aim a kick at the cat when we jam a finger."

"It was more than that. She never forgave me."

"No, Benny, it was herself she never forgave. I don't doubt for a minute she made life pretty rough for you, but you were just the cat – just a reminder."

"If I'd only been the cat I'd have only got the kick on her bad days, when something went wrong. In between we could have lived reasonably happy lives, like other families. But the Sunday clothes and the bow ties went on for years. I even used to sniffle and blubber sometimes, beg her, and she'd just set her mouth. Right to the last she was trying to get even."

"Put yourself in her place. She'd slipped, with the town looking on. No place to hide. It's still bad enough, they still smack their lips when they catch somebody; but thirty years ago it was a lot worse."

"At least she did a good job on me. She didn't even have to stick it out. I was only eleven and her work was done."

"Remember that part of the job was to make you a musician. You don't regret that, do you?"

"In fact she'd be wild if she knew – ready to rip my eyes out. Something that I liked, that gave me a living – oh no, that wasn't what she intended. I turned the tables on her. I'd like to see her face."

"Come off it, Benny. She was an unhappy woman, she wasn't a monster."

"When is a monster not a monster? Those music lessons – maybe you remember old Phyllis Devine, with the red wig. Fifty cents for half an hour – she had her shingle out, just a few doors up the street – but that was too easy. After a few months she wasn't good enough for Mrs. Fox's little boy. Upward size, no background – that wig – so every Saturday, bow tie and shiny music satchel, away went Benny to Comet for his lesson. Maybe you knew, or heard. Or more likely you had other things on your mind. It started when I was eight. I'd catch the train here in the morning at eleven and be in Comet about twelve. With sandwiches in my satchel and fifteen cents for a bowl of soup at the

Chinese restaurant. Something hot on my stomach. A good mother – nobody could say she neglected her little boy. Along with the soup the Chinaman used to give me a piece of raisin pie and a cup of coffee. Buddies – he used to call me Benny Flox. His name was Sam, and when I told him my father's name was Sam too the bond was sealed. But even more important than the pie and coffee, he used to let me sit – lesson time was half-past three. The teacher was a Mrs. Gracey – very good, no wig. She used to let me sit too if I wasn't in the way, but her waiting-room wasn't very big, just a little hall outside the living-room where she gave the lessons, and Saturday of course was her busy day. So I'd go for a walk, usually up the track a piece where no one could see me, and end up waiting a couple of hours in the station. If I'd managed to scrape up an extra dime of my own during the week I'd go back to Sam's for lemonade or ice cream and sit there again. A nice long lazy day – the train back was at seven . . . . For more than three years, until the day of the pills, when everybody was happily released."

"Sam never stepped in, never tried to talk sense to her?"

"Well, he of course had violated her. You know, got into her. Poor innocent girl away from home. He'd persuaded her to spread her legs for him. And so help me she'd worn him down to the point where he felt just about as guilty as I did. So he never fought back. Anything for peace – only of course he never got peace."

"But Benny, she's been dead twenty years. Why keep it alive, why go on tormenting yourself?"

"Tormenting myself? Oh no, nothing like that. I'm the most popular fellow in Upward, haven't you heard? Friendly, lots of fun, easy to get along with – Benny can liven up the dullest evening. Everybody knows about him, everybody winks behind his back. Sometimes he catches them, but nobody minds. A very broad-minded town – musicians, you know, a lot of them are like that. Right now after the Hospital Dance and his generous contribution he's riding especially high. At the same time nobody wants to be seen getting too friendly with him. Walking up the street together, having a coffee – at least not too often. Three or four's all right. Safety in numbers, they can protect one another. Even Stan – and who in Upward is above the breath of suspicion if not a Gillespie? – even he's careful . . . . At that, Benny does get around – you'd be surprised – but the watchword is discretion."

"Years ago, Benny, the first time we talked, I told you to get out of Upward. I still think you should."

"I remember. Father had been to see you, scared I wasn't turning out normal – right? Maybe you could have a little talk with him – right? And you were one in a million, I'll always be grateful. You didn't suggest baseball or a prayer session with the preacher or tell me to think manly thoughts. You said get out."

"You're what – thirty-two? At my age that seems just a boy – a long life ahead of you. Of course you should get out – Upward's a fish bowl. The day may come when somebody forgets to be discreet and then it may be dangerous. I'm not much help – I'll admit I don't understand – but you've a right to live your own life, the way you want to live it."

"The trouble is I'm still wearing the bow ties."

"Well, Nick had the boots and the fur cap. Don't spend too much time feeling sorry for yourself."

"That first talk we had – I think I was twenty, twenty-one – I took it to heart, you know. I don't suppose you kept an eye on me but a few months later – maybe six, I had to save for it – I took a little trip. Chicago – a holiday, to hear some of the big bands, maybe get some ideas. But actually of course I went to explore, see what things were really like out there, in my country.

"Beginner's luck: the first night I made out famously. Boy, was this the life, and was it easy! And Benny Fox from Upward, Saskatchewan, did he know how to handle himself! The next night, taking a bit too much for granted, Benny read the signals wrong and got himself punched out. His wallet disappeared too, with about half his money. So for the next two weeks what did he do? Lived on beans and hot dogs and spent a very dull time watching cheap movies while his lip and eye returned to normal. Then he came back to Upward to tell about the wonders of the big city and the time he'd had."

"What about Sam? Any idea what he thinks?"

"I know what you mean – the father of the queer wore a brave, embarrassed smile. Wouldn't getting out make things easier for him. But surprisingly he's very proud of me. When there's a dance he comes over to the hall sometimes and sits at the back listening. If I can get down for a few minutes to have a Coke with him you should see his face – on the top of the world. He still feels so guilty about what he did to *her*. I sort of make it up to him."

"He could be just as proud if you were playing in a band somewhere else. It's your life."

"I know. I keep thinking about those hot dogs."

"Chicago and the hot dogs were beginner's luck, just as you say. Bad luck – you ought to have sense enough to know. I mean get away for good, make a new life. I don't know what kind of musician you are – you sound fine to me – but at least you should be able to get by. Take your time, settle in, make friends—"

"And learn to read the signals."

"Why not? What I'm afraid of is that some day you'll read them wrong here."

"I know – sometimes I have bad dreams."

"Just in case, Benny, always be sure you have a little money put by. It's an old man talking, so don't mind. The more the better – and above all, don't let anybody know you've got it."

"For a fast get-away. I know, I've thought of it – before they arrive with the tar pot and pillows. . . . But right now I'm taking up too much of your time. There are half a dozen waiting to talk to you. I'm getting some dirty looks."

"And I'd better get on my feet again – when I'm up I can handle them faster."

"Doc, is there anything you'd like me to play? Any particular old song? It's probably the last time you'll hear your piano."

"Don't suppose you know an old one called *Redwing*?"

"Well, It's your paper Nellie, but since you're asking me I'll tell you straight I don't see why. Mind you now I'm not against her – not real dead set against her. I always say hello Maisie, how are things, and I've even stopped a couple of times and said why don't you come to church because I know Grimble keeps after her and somebody else speaking up too might be just what she needs to bring her round. But writing a piece about her in the paper, making a big to-do – well, no, I can't say I think it's wise."

"It's just that all these years she's been filling in – a wonderful job and never a word of thanks. I mean what would we have done while we were waiting?"

"We'd probably have done just fine – maybe a lot better. Sure she's been doing a job, earning a living the same as the rest of us. Do you really think if it hadn't been her parlour it wouldn't have been somebody else's? She got started first, that was all. Doc gave her a hand."

"There's something to be said, though, for service, and anyone who's ever stayed with her will tell you how good she was. Kept everything so clean—"

"Yes, Nellie, but one way or another don't we all give service? The stores and the station and the telephone – you and Dan. What's so special about keeping clean sheets on four or five beds and emptying a few bed pans?"

"What I mean, all these years we've snubbed her, and yet we've been glad to have her on hand, ready to use her—"

"If the town snubbed her it was for a good reason. Let's face it – wouldn't a lot of us like a change now and then? Talk about service – isn't putting up with what we've got, our Dans and our Dicks, listening to their grouches, admiring their bulges, isn't that service?"

"It's not quite the same. We've *got* our Dans and Dicks."

"And why hasn't she got her whatever his name was? Because a few months after they were married he caught her in the act and walked out. Not a word, just packed a bag and she never saw him again."

"I know, I've heard about it too. But even if she had it coming to her, it was such a long time ago. All these years she's been paying—"

"All these years she's been making out fairly well. Never lonely. Doc, you know, wasn't the only one, oh no, there's a lot would swear to that. And not killing herself either. She could always afford a girl to help her, she wasn't the one who emptied the bed pans."

"Oh dear, it's just that I've always felt so sorry. You'll admit she's never exactly brazened it out. If she sees you and has time she ducks around a corner. It hurts – you can see it in her face. And we don't know – maybe it's something she can't help. We're not all made the same."

"Indeed, we're not, but let's be blunt about it – the difference isn't in how much we want a man between our legs as in how much we respect ourselves."

"I suppose you're right. We just thought it would be rather nice to let her know that despite everything the town's not all against her. Now that the hospital's opening and there'll be no more need of her beds—"

"There are a lot it would be nice to write up, Nellie. A lot of farm women – a lot of us who came through the bad years and managed to keep a home together and our families fed and warm. I'm not saying Maisie maybe hasn't got her good points and I'm not saying either like some of them have said that she ought to have been run out of town years ago, but haven't we all got our good points, don't we all do a job?"

"It would be a gesture, though. It wouldn't hurt us. We've not shown much charity over the years. We've been smug and self-righteous and some of us maybe have done things just as bad."

"Nellie, it's your paper. I'm only speaking out because you've asked me, because we're old friends. But stop and think a minute – what's your gesture going to do for *her*? Just remind people, start up all the old talk—"

"It might at least make a few take an interest – let bygones be bygones. She's been an outcast long enough."

"Fine, by all means take an interest, but Grimble's got the right idea. Talk her into coming to church, that's the way to do it. The first time or two I'd even walk in with her myself. People wouldn't forget but they wouldn't mind so much once they saw she'd come round."

"In other words, once they saw she had repented, admitted the error of her ways."

"And what's wrong with repentance, Nellie? A little of it, I daresay, would be good for us all."

"She, though, has to do hers publicly—"

"Well, isn't it the way she's done everything else?"

"Stan, do you know *Redwing*? An old one, Doc's asking for it."

"Whistle a bit, I'm not sure."

"I'll keep it low—"

"Maybe, sounds familiar. A little more—"

"You don't know the words? I think it starts *There once was an Indian maid*—"

"*Who went to the bush and got laid.* Sure I know them."

"Brilliant, you're getting better. There's Mrs. Billy – and Mrs. Jack – I wonder if they do."

"Watch it. They don't speak."

"Doesn't matter. Maybe we can all sing . . . . Mrs. Billy, do you know an old one called *Redwing*?"

"Of course I know *Redwing*. My mother used to sing it—

Now, now the sun shines bright on Redwing,
My pretty Redwing—"

"Good, you know the words then—"

"Oh no, I don't think so. Just *my pretty Redwing*—"

"Mrs. Jack, do you know *Redwing*?"

"Of course I know *Redwing*. Years and years ago when I was

a little girl we had a record. A cylinder record, remember? One of those old Edison machines."

"You know the words?"

"Let me think—

>Far far away her brave is sleeping,
>And Redwing's weeping
>Her heart away—

Something like that."

"Well, maybe Nellie does. Psst, Nellie, come over here a minute. Do you know a song called *Redwing*? An old one—"

"Of course I know Redwing. We used to sing it at school. It was all the rage—

>There once was an Indian maid,
>A shy little maid of old—"

"You know the words then?"

"Oh dear, it's such a long time—

>The sun is shining
>And Redwing's pining
>Her heart away—

Something like that."

"Oh yes, Benny, I've just remembered. There's another bit that goes—

>Her brave is dying,
>And Redwing's sighing—"

"But that can't be right. If she's *weeping when he's sleeping* she wouldn't just be *sighing when he's dying*."

"Maybe because he's not sleeping with her. I suppose it happened sometimes with the Indians too."

"And your bit, Nellie, doesn't make sense either – *The sun is shining and Redwing's pining.* Why should she be pining when the sun is shining, what's the connection?"

"Perhaps it's intended as a comment on the indifference of nature to the human predicament. Very Canadian."

"At least we all know the tune, so let's try. All three of you, sing as many words as you know and fill in the rest with Indian."

"But we don't know Indian!"

"What difference does that make? Mrs. Billy, you're soprano, so do a sort of obbligato – Sioux or Blackfoot, suit yourself. And you, Stan, and Mrs. Jack, when you run out of words just fill in with the drums – you know, *A shy little maid of old, tum tum, Tum tum tum warrior bold* – and then every so often come in strong with *Redwing.*"

"But they'll think we're crazy!"

"Well—"

"It's *Redwing*, Nellie, isn't that wonderful? They're singing *Redwing.* Did you tell them?"

"No, Benny just wanted to know if I remembered the words. Doc must have asked for it."

"I must say they're not singing it very well. Poor Edith!"

"I wonder what Mrs. Billy's trying to do. It's so wobbly, and high—"

"Well, it's an Indian song, so maybe she intends it as an Indian love call. Or a prayer for rain."

"And look, Rose, what on earth is Stanley doing with his hips?"

"Yes, I see what you mean . . . and he's certainly got it wrong. Our Indians were a brave and noble people. A Leaping Buffalo or a Lean Coyote would never wriggle like that."

"Tear your eyes away a minute and look at poor brother Duncan."

"Smiling bravely through. I wonder why he doesn't kill him."

"They say his big number with Benny's band this spring is *Don't Fence Me In.*"

"I know, and can you imagine anybody wanting to!"

"Poor Doc – he has his hand over his eyes."

"Of course, he's been standing. Perhaps he's just tired."

"When I think of the way she had the music on the piano that day, set out so carefully, making sure we'd all see it—"

"At last! Oh look, Nellie – isn't that nice of him, Doc's clapping too."

"What's Benny up to now? He and Mrs. Billy – I'm afraid they're going to do another . . . . I suppose we'll have to put all this in the *Chronicle* and Dan hasn't left himself much space – 'An impromptu trio provided a spirited rendering of *Redwing*, with special love-call effects by Mrs. Billy.'"

"Just don't forget that if you say 'special effects by Mrs. Billy' you'll have to add, 'supported by Mrs. Jack's rich contralto.'"

"*When You Come to the End of a Perfect Day*—Oh dear, I thought that one was safely buried years ago, although in a way I suppose it's appropriate."

"Mrs. Billy and Mrs. Jack certainly don't look as if it's been a perfect day for them. Did you ever see such faces? Getting them to sing together I'm afraid ends nothing."

"No more than does poor Doc's departure. Good old Upward marches on."

Then, at the beginning, maybe then if I had tried – tried harder, tried again, yes maybe then – but in the beginning how can you take time? How can you think of someone you marry as a case? You don't hold clinics in the bridal bed.

Not so young either, thirty thirty-one, and still the calf-eyed stage, she loves me loves me not, like a little girl with daisies plucking petals twenty times a day. It was different fifty years ago – you sighed and waited, mooned. Even a doctor – you cherished smiles and photographs, the brush of hands. Queen was the word – in the country of the lover there is no excess – and when at last the night of nights and she withdrawn, wincing as if assaulted by a horror, snout and fangs, how know it was not rejection but a case? After the smiles and promises, the glow, the promises of warmth, how not believe encountering the cold that I, a clod, had failed her? How guess the queen was cornered and at bay? In the master moment of possession how diagnose an abnormality, how plot a cure? The moment of the body's great white light – how know that not disdain was snuffing it, nor disillusionment, but the gutter from some tainted memory, some childhood dread? Nobody tells you even a bride can be a case.

Not many nights – the night of the moon, spread out exposed and shining, throat drawn and corded, straining away as if to clear a kink, the mouth a wince of outrage, ravished bride and I the loathsome ravisher, that was not many nights . . . The little spasm of rattler fury, retaliative, coiled then sprung, muscles and pride contracted in withdrawal, not even time to bring it to an end – withdrawal and a slap of silence, stalking off if that's how it is then there are other rooms, yes, other bodies too, you'll see, affronted dignity tight like a towel around my loins . . . Night of the moon, the night I saw, and not another word until the day she died, just the weather and the roast, if there are any calls you can tell them I'll be back by three . . .

Redwing Redwing – of all the silly damfool songs what did I ask him that one for? She used to hammer away at it so loud and slow, she seemed to think *and Redwing's weeping her heart away.*

"Coffee, Ladies and Gentlemen – coffee, coffee. It's ready, waiting for you now downstairs. Coffee and sandwiches, but you're not all to rush at once. You hear now, just two or three at a time and steady. There's no place to eat and drink down there so come back and do it up here. But when you've finished you're not to put your cups and saucers on the floor. Bring them over here, right where I'm standing, and put them on this table. You hear now. If you put them on the floor you'll forget, nothing's surer, and then put your feet on them or back up a chair. All the coffee and sandwiches you want, don't be shy about coming back for more. There's ham sandwiches and chopped egg sandwiches and salmon sandwiches and some other kind that's sort of chopped-looking too. A couple of tubfuls. We don't want anybody going home from Doc's party hungry. Just don't forget about putting your dishes on the floor and then putting your feet on the dishes. We're going to have enough mess to clean up as it is.

"There's doughnuts too—"

"You mean, Dan, have I often tried my hand at playing God?"

"Well, isn't it true there are times when every doctor finds himself on the spot, a decision to make? In the old days it must have been especially hard – everything new and raw, not much interference, nothing but your little black bag and your conscience."

"Most of the time I just played safe and followed the rules. Took the easy way, made my decisions by the book."

"You say most of the time. Does that mean—"

"Not much to tell you, Dan, that would make the front page of the *Chronicle*. In the old days, remember, there was their conscience too, more of it than now. I suppose I leaned on it."

"You mean they bowed their heads and said Thy will be done?"

"Well, miracles weren't expected of a doctor. He was just there to help. *For man is born unto trouble* – they had it in their bones. They gritted their teeth, hung on till it was time."

"So if you did make a decision you were completely on your own?"

"Sometimes even though they didn't expect a decision they wanted it. And needed it. So that I wasn't completely on my own."

"Sometimes, in other words, you sensed they were with you, ahead of you—"

"Someone's dying – say a woman looking up at you with a pair of cancer eyes – you don't have to do much sensing."

"And afterwards? A feeling you'd done the right thing? Doubts?"

"If anything ever kept me awake it was for having hesitated, held back, not the other way. I can still remember in fact the first time, the relief when I did decide."

"The woman with the cancer?"

"Fifteen minutes, maybe just five, but I was new and raw, a long time ago, and it seemed like that many years. Her husband hadn't come for me till it was pretty well all over. Even with the kind of examination I could give her in the shack I knew she had six weeks at the longest. She'd always been a whiner, he explained, always something wrong with her. How was he to know? Meals and cows and children right up to the day she caved in. A hot dirty little shack, dirty bedclothes, the usual salt pork – a twelve-year-old neighbour girl rushed over to help – so I lit into him and said she had less than a week. Too late to think of the hospital in Comet – fifteen miles and the shape she was in she'd never stand it. Gave her some morphine, came back, and instead of six weeks, just as I had told him, she lasted less than one . . . . Shouldn't be telling that, but I don't suppose it matters now. More than forty years ago – too late for them to take away my practice."

"Considering the circumstances, it's hard to believe they would have taken it away even then . . . . And the husband, I suppose he didn't put up much resistance – I mean about getting her to the hospital?"

"He wasn't a bad fellow – just another dry year. The sight of the woman made me jump on him – yellow, skin and bones – but of course she hadn't got that way overnight. Time for him to get used to it. You don't notice changes when they're small and slow. The hospital would have only meant spinning it out, spinning out the pain too. They wouldn't have given her enough morphine – and a bill for him of maybe two or three hundred dollars. And that was part of the decision. He had enough on his hands – three or four of a family, a lot of stones and sand."

"You say relief, so you must have felt you had done the right thing. Well then, wasn't the power to do it a temptation? In those days I don't suppose there was much risk of anyone poking around and starting inquiries."

"Scared the daylights out of me. Not so much that time as a year or so later, a fellow with a pitchfork in his belly."

"Self-inflicted?"

"With a pitchfork? He'd have needed a long arm. No, if it had ever got to court I suppose they'd have called it attempted rape and manslaughter – one in fact that just might have made the *Chronicle*. A bachelor, at least fifty, who'd tried to get a bit too friendly with his neighbour's daughter. She fought him off and ran, and not surprisingly her father strode over in a fine state of righteous wrath to warn what would happen the next time. But instead of being ashamed or apologetic the fellow turned on him and tried to put the blame on the girl. It was in the stable and he had a pitchfork in his hands. He pointed it, accusingly I suppose – cheap little slut, why don't you bring her up properly, something like that – and the father grabbed it away and gave him a jab in the belly."

"And then panicked and came for you?"

"Not right away – he thought he'd just nicked him – and it was noon the next day before I got there. There was nothing I could do, but he knew I was the doctor and he could still talk a little. Don't tell the Mounties, that was the message. His father was still living, somewhere in Manitoba, and he didn't want him to know. In other words, so far as he was concerned, he'd only got what was coming to him."

"Case closed, then—"

"Well, supposing I'd reported it to the Mounties – they'd have taken the father in and eventually there'd have been a trial. They might have believed his story, but still it would have been manslaughter, and he'd have probably got four or five years. The other neighbours weren't in danger – he wasn't the killer type – and he had his family. Early August, just about time to cut the crop—"

"And since there had been a kind of rough justice—"

"It was such an easy decision, in the circumstances so right."

"So easy and right you were afraid you might get in the habit?"

"Back in town after I'd signed the death certificate – after I'd faked it, in fact – it struck me that without batting an eye I'd taken it on myself to be judge too. What we call the normal processes of law – why bother? Wasn't Doc Hunter doing all right? I suppose you could say I've always had a practical, commonsense way of looking at things – even a fairly decent way – but what about another time, a case not so simple and clearcut? And as you say, no interference, no one to dispute the doctor's word."

"You saw where you were heading and then pulled back . . . never took it on yourself again to make a decision?"

"I didn't say that. I just said decisions sometimes scared me."

"But the woman with the cancer and the man with the pitchfork in his belly – when you look back your conscience doesn't bother you?"

"As I say, they were easy."

"The others, then—"

"Well, I can think of two others that were easy – no regrets, no reproaches – and another that's left just the ghost of a doubt."

"Four out of five. Not a bad score."

"One of the easy ones is no secret. Cliff Dean – remember, he shot himself? – and the girl, Della something, who had a bad attack of bronchitis just about that time and spent a few days with Maisie. She said nobody knew – except Cliff, of course – and then it turned out she'd told a couple of her friends. Well, that kind of news spreads fast, so when the pregnancy didn't develop Upward naturally started to wonder about the attack of bronchitis."

"I remember – lots of talk but not much criticism. Pretty well everyone, I think, was on your side."

"You should see her now – big farm on the other side of Comet, four or five boys. The size of all outdoors – arms on her like hams – and at the time she looked so scared and wispy. Eyes bigger than all the rest of her. Misery piled on misery. Seventeen

– her first time round. She loved the man, she was carrying his child, and because of it he'd blown out his brains."

"If the body's given a chance it cures itself, right? A cut heals, we get over a cold. You'd say the same about the mind? The same recuperative power?"

"Given a chance . . . . One of the other decisions I mentioned, they came through too, both of them, and the fix they were in was a lot worse. Talk about a pair of eyes and misery—"

"Both of them, you say – then whose eyes?"

"It was the girl's father who came to see me. Just the day before, that was what brought him, he'd caught himself thinking of killing her. They had a well with a rope and pulley – he'd watched her pulling up water and it struck him how easy it would be to push her in and make it look as if she'd jumped."

"Because she was going to have a baby?"

"I said can't you get the man to marry her? Wouldn't answer – just the eyes. Is he married already? No answer. Dead? No answer, still just the eyes, and then believe it or not he went down on his knees."

"He was the one?"

"And somehow it wasn't nearly as bad as it sounds. I know, you couldn't give him very high marks for moral principles or control, but for the life of you you couldn't write him off as a degenerate either. The girl was important to him, and I mean in the right way. His wife had died a few years before; now she was his whole life. It sounds crazy, but in so many ways he was a good father."

"What about wanting to throw her down the well? You think that had just been to play on your sympathy?"

"No, he impressed me as a fairly simple, straightforward fellow. I think more likely he was genuinely scared he might."

"And if you hadn't helped out?"

"Not his own daughter. Not when the moment came. He'd never have gone that far."

"He'd already gone a fair distance, just the same—"

"Oh yes, I was shocked too – not nearly so tough as I am now – but somehow it all fell into place when I saw the curtain. Faded green, with little yellow roses – strung on a bit of cord – a big dip. Just the two of them, eighteen and forty. She was a pretty girl, well developed, nice walk, and he was a young forty. Often in the old homestead days a man would let himself go – slouch and sour. Shave once a week, clean shirt once a week, smile once a week – some weeks. But this fellow had hung on better. He still had ideas about himself, careful, trim. That fall they'd had a fire and the house was pretty well gutted, so they'd been getting through the winter in just the one room. Stove, table, chairs, the beds side by side with just the curtain – you can imagine."

"And they came through all right?"

"She stayed on a while working for Maisie – my terms were separation, no repeat performances. Then I found a job for her a few towns up the line, somebody I knew that had a store, and about a year later she married a commercial traveller. Went to live in Winnipeg – apparently no harm done. He married too, and had two more girls. For years he brought me a turkey at Christmas. Maisie used to be glad of it . . . . Yes, I'd say they came through all right. One of the things, in fact, I'm glad I had a chance to do."

"But there's another you say that left a doubt?"

"Shoe on the other foot – that time I said no."

"Caution? Or a decision?"

"No, the lady riled me. Bossy, as if that was what I was there for. When I tried to reason with her, pointing out all the things against it, she cut me short. That was her concern, she didn't care to discuss it. All she wanted was my services and she was prepared to pay. Well, I opened the door for her and said Good Afternoon and a couple of days she was back, all apologies but the same attitude – just my professional services, please, no moralizing or advice. So I said Good Afternoon again and then she lit into me, both barrels. Didn't I realize what I was doing, ruining her life—"

"All right, she riled you, got under your skin – but wouldn't your answer have been the same anyway? I don't imagine you made a practice of going along with that kind of request."

"Well, if I hadn't got riled, I might have listened."

"You mean there were special circumstances? Something over and above the usual story of innocence betrayed?"

"Special circumstances, Dan, can sometimes be just the thickness of the skin. The bossy tone that irritated me – if I'd listened I might have understood that hers was dangerously thin."

"And realized that she was one whose chances of coming through weren't good?"

"It's a bad spot for any girl – she's bound to have a rough time – but for one it's a rough time and for another it's the end of the road."

"I gather that's what it was for her?"

"Yes, she suffered and eventually she cracked. And along the way she made others suffer too."

"Then why do you say only a ghost of a doubt. Why wasn't it an out-and-out wrong decision?"

"Well, the child was born . . . . Life for him hasn't been a bed of roses either. You could make a case easy enough that it would have been better, and yet I'm sort of glad that he's around."

"Excuse me, Doctor, I've brought you a cup of coffee and some sandwiches. Egg, ham, salmon, one of each. I'll be back in a few minutes to see how you're getting along."

"Well, here's one pair of eyes that won't be brimming when they see the last of Sawbones. No money for the druggist in salt."

"Good gargle, just the same. Better than all your fancy pink and green stuff in bottles. Good for the teeth, too."

"Just think though all these years how you could have been boosting my profits, to say nothing of the morale of your patients. There's a psychological angle. Who gets a lift out of being told to go home and gargle with salt? Think of the money we could both have made if you'd worked with me."

"I'll tell Nick to expect some feelers, and to strike a hard bargain."

"No feelers. I just hope he's not another salt and aspirin man. It's nearly time I had a new car."

"You'll get your car, Alex – the future's yours. It's all drugs these days. You should see the samples that keep coming in from the laboratories. Makes you dizzy just trying to keep track of which does what. Penicillin's barely the beginning. Before long they're even going to have a contraceptive pill – that's right, by mouth, they're working on it – and think how that'll keep your cash register clanging."

"My boy's fourteen – the other day we were talking about the new man, some of the stories, and now he and a couple of his friends have decided they want to be doctors too. The idea's getting to be fashionable. His mother's sort of a church woman and she's been thinking all along it might be nice to have a preacher in the family, but he's let her know what she can do with that one."

"It's a good time – new drugs, new everything. Now that it's all over it seems I've never done anything but deliver babies and set a few broken bones. As you say, a salt and aspirin man. I sort of envy Nick."

"So why not stay on with him a couple of years? Plenty to keep you both busy, everybody itching to try the new hospital."

"I've overstayed as it is. I forget things, my hands aren't as steady as they should be, I've got a cataract on the way."

"But you don't have to take your troubles to Saskatoon. Never mind your niece. Upward's where you belong."

"When you're seventy-five, Alex, and your work's behind you, you don't really belong anywhere. You're just taking up space."

"Come off it. It's just all these damned good-byes, they're getting you down. In the morning you'll feel like twenty-five again."

"Years ago, before your time, I used to take Nick with me sometimes on a call – he liked to watch. Dunc Gillespie too, but Nick was a better watcher. It was more important to him. He knew *what* to watch. Sometimes I'd let him help, hold things – pretend to let him help. Now every so often he'd probably remember to return the favour – ask me to drop round to see a patient, what do I think? That sort of thing, so I'd still feel important too . . . . No, I'd rather mumble and nod among strangers."

"But what are you going to do with yourself all day in the meantime, till you've reached the mumbling and nodding stage?"

"Well, my niece has a house – out a piece, she says, with a big garden – and I think she's got plans for me. Hoeing potatoes, I suppose, and mowing the lawn. And I'm going to get a dog, maybe a pair. I may even start raising them. I'd rather have horses – they're fussier about where and what they lick – but in the city of course there would be problems."

"You could raise horses here."

"I said I'd like to raise them – but apart from the problems, there wouldn't be much sense. Who wants or needs horses to-day? At least you can sell Labradors or shepherds. Pretend you're doing something."

"Maybe I'll be your first customer. Let me know. I want a good duck dog."

"At that I'm not sure. It may keep me busy fighting with my niece. And training her. Damned fool of a woman if ever there was one. She's got a ouija board and talks to her dead husband. When she was here last fall that was all she wanted to do. He was having trouble getting through, couldn't get beamed in on Upward."

"Excuse me, Doctor, how are the sandwiches? More coffee?"

"You can take these two back and bring me another ham. More mustard and the coffee black this time."

"Well, I'll ask to be sure, but somebody made the sandwiches at home so I'm afraid there's no mustard."

"Doesn't matter. I'll have another anyway."

"Two ham sandwiches with mustard at eleven o'clock at night plus two cups of coffee – remember the lecture you gave me the last time I was in your office about weight control and keeping my pressure down? No stimulants, the danger of overtaxing my heart?"

"You're what? Close to fifty? Well then, you can't afford two ham sandwiches with mustard plus two cups of coffee. Especially the way your pot's coming along."

"And at seventy-five you can? No danger of overtaxing your heart?"

"Maybe, but at seventy-five what's wrong with a good heart attack?"

"Say that again—"

"Well, let's not play games with ourselves. We've got to go and at seventy-five we've got to go fairly soon. Two, five, ten years – the Lord deliver us, maybe even twenty – but the sentence is going to be carried out. And wouldn't you just as soon have a firing squad as the rats taking their time. You've still got a long way to go, a lot of work ahead of you, that boy—"

"You don't mean you're doing this deliberately?"

"If I wanted to get it over with, Alex, I wouldn't fool around with mustard and coffee. I just say that for an old man a heart attack isn't the worst thing. I can't see the point of making life miserable trying to play safe – doing without salt, living on soft-boiled eggs and prunes and a cup of weak tea."

"Yes, but that's going against nature. Right to the last there's the will to live."

"Well, we may win a stay of execution with the soft-boiled eggs and prunes; we may even be lucky and in a weak-tea sort of way enjoy ourselves for a few years. But as I say, the reprieve is often just time for the rats to get in."

"You're thinking of cancer?"

"Among other things. Myself, for instance, I never get through the night without two or three trips to the bathroom. But I'm lucky, as yet. Old men are often up every hour. Often they lose control altogether, of everything. Don't you think a heart attack – maybe a bad five or ten minutes – would be better?"

"Here are the sandwiches, Doctor, and there's mustard after all. But it's the hot kind so you'd better put it on yourself. I've brought a knife."

"That's the kind I like. Just leave it here, I'll manage fine."

"I see what you mean – *he who fights and runs away*. It's just that you're always reading about heart disease, the worst killer."

"The same as you're always hearing jokes about an old man's sex life. He tries so hard to get it up, and then when he makes it he takes so long – as if not being able to get it up was the worst thing that could happen to him, the last turn of the knife. But what about success? Don't you think that might be an even worse humiliation?"

"You'll have to explain that one for me."

"Look at our old friend Harry Hubbs over there. Every time he sees you he tells you he's still got all his teeth, which probably means he hasn't got much else. A sort of compensation – trying to convince himself he's still in there holding his own with the young fellows. But supposing the miracle happens some day and he does get it up. What's he going to do with it?"

"Just the same it's something pretty important to a man. I don't see where the humiliation would come in."

"The look in the lady's eyes. Supposing he were to knock at her door and say see what I've got . . . . But, Alex, what I've got to get up right now is my state of mind, from sex to things of the spirit if I can manage it. The Reverend Grimble has had a Day-of-Reckoning eye on me all evening and now I think he's moving in for the kill. How many years is it he's been in Upward – ten, twelve? And I haven't set foot inside his church once."

"Benny, will you do something for me? We've got a watch for Doc and I'm elected to make the presentation speech but I'm worried. He looks tired and he may just choke up and stand there."

"Doc choke up? In public? A fine judge of character you are!"

"I'm not so sure – leaving a town after forty-five years can't be easy. Anyway, I want you to sit down at the piano and be ready, just in case. If he gets flustered or looks as if he might break down, I'll give you the signal and start in fast with *For He's A Jolly Good Fellow*. I've spoken to Stan and Mrs. Jack so they'll be ready to join in. But not unless I give the signal. He likely suspects a presentation and he may have a half-hour speech all memorized."

"Just see to it, my dear Mr. President, that *your* speech isn't half an hour. That I simply could not stand. Half a minute will be plenty."

"There's Grimble, dammit, moving in on him. As soon as he's finished—"

"You say you're not a religious man, Doctor, and while I can't for the life of me think of you as an irreligious one, I respect your outlook, but at the same time I'm curious. For roughly fifty years you've been a practising physician, working close to the bone, life and death, suffering, defeat: now that it's all behind you, can you sum it up?"

"That's a tall order, Mr. Grimble. You should have warned me a month ago."

"I'm not trying to extract a little nugget of wisdom or philosophy for Sunday's sermon. It's for myself, my own satisfaction. When you say you're not a religious man, I suppose you mean you're what is popularly called a rationalist: well then, when you look at life and death rationally, what do you make of them?"

"Long ago I gave up trying to make anything of them. As you say, I've been a practising doctor; my time has been pretty well taken up with the practical problems of the job. Helping a child to be born – that kind of problem – doing what I could to make sure it was born alive and well, with a fair chance of survival; I never took it on myself to ask if it was worth keeping alive."

"Yet you must have had your own thoughts. I'm sure you never just let your mind go blank."

"Well, as you know, a doctor is trained in the traditions of healing, and along with them, I suppose, goes an assumption that life is important, worth saving. But I've never taken a very hard look at that one either. It always just seemed to make sense."

"And you leave it there? You're content to leave it there?"

"I'm not a religious man, I'm not an intellectual. Where can I take it?"

"You keep saying you're not a religious man and yet you accept the value and importance of life. There seems to be a contradiction. The little span of life we know – birth to death – what possible value or importance can it have if there's no before or after?"

"The value and importance we give it, I suppose . . . but apart from that, when a man is suffering you don't take time to think about before and after. You think only about him."

"Yes, but if you think about him only rationally he's such an improbable creature. You've already said it yourself: he doesn't come into the world just to feed and beget and die, but also to establish these traditions of healing and responsibility, to make sacrifices, build ideals. Do you think his being that way is just a matter of chance? A lucky throw? Doesn't it suggest there must be a plan, a purpose? That somewhere in the background there's an Intelligence?"

"An Intelligence, yes. A purpose or plan, I'm not convinced."

"But surely if there's an Intelligence—"

"I know, another contradiction. I suppose that's why I gave up."

"You think then this Intelligence exists apart, in isolation, self-absorbed? Without before or after either? Blind and aimless, yet an Intelligence?"

"I'm afraid I'm out of my depth, Mr. Grimble. My thinking along these lines isn't very well ordered. What I'm trying to say is there seems so much intelligence – the evidence is everywhere – and at the same time such a lack of it. So many miracles—"

"Ah-ha! Isn't that a strange word for a man who insists he's not religious?"

"I'm not thinking of biblical miracles – water into wine, that sort of thing . . . . A bird, say, or an anthill or a little garter snake – or take the bird in your hand and stretch out the wing. Expert jobs, all so beautifully fitted. I agree it's hard to believe that they too are just what you call lucky throws—"

"Of course, nothing could be more obvious. So why talk about

Intelligence and at the same time the lack of It? How can It be and at the same time not be?"

"Well, It might *be*, all right, but not be here."

"The miracles, though, the snakes and birds – they're here."

"But the Mind or Will that's responsible – It might have left, decided this wasn't the place."

"I'm sorry, Doctor, I was serious. But I suppose a little fare-well gathering isn't the time or place."

"I'm serious too, now that you've got me started. This Will or Intelligence goes to such trouble, works with such skill, such awareness, and then seems to forget, or at least to lose interest. Take ants. What an enormous amount of creative intelligence has been spent on them, and where are they going?"

"But ants are just ants. Does it matter very much where they're going?"

"And yet they're one of the miracles. Instincts, defences, or-ganization, and all for what? Millions of years they just keep on being ants."

"Yes, Doctor, but I don't think we should be too pessimistic about life or the universe just because ants keep on being ants. I suppose something went wrong in their development. There are other forms of life."

"Ourselves, for instance. And where are we off to?"

"Well, you only have to think of ancient peoples or primitives, say our own Indians, and then make comparisons."

"With what? Their war dances with some of the things we've been up to during the last four or five years?"

"And yet the horrors may have taught us something. We do have the capacity to learn, to improve. And after all, humanity is greater than a handful of butchers or the miseries and exigen-cies of a war."

"What about a handful of saints? Doesn't humanity do a pretty good job of holding its own against them too? Taking the long view, after two thousand years—"

"Like the ants, you mean, no progress, the same repetition – oh no."

"Like the ants and the flies and the crows – doctors trying to heal bodies, priests and preachers trying to heal souls – all miracles, all going nowhere. Creation one day, destruction the next – a sort of game – like turning out jugs and bowls just to be able to have the fun of smashing them."

"No, no, Doctor. Why, take your own forty-five years in Upward—"

"I remember once long ago reading about a tribe somewhere that believed in a Great Sow that eats her own farrow. Nearly made me throw up, and yet maybe they were on to it. The Great Mother and the Evil Mother, maybe one and the same, creating life only to turn and destroy it . . . . As if the potter got his wheel going and then couldn't stop it – and not knowing what to do with all the jugs and bottles piling up, no storage space, no markets, had to rig up another machine to grind them into dust again."

"But the very absurdity of such a thought – creative intelligence on the one side and mindless destruction on the other – doesn't it suggest it's our view of things which is at fault? The universe, the scheme of things, it's not concerned about what we think, whether we understand or not. It goes its own way, inscrutable. It doesn't feel it owes us an explanation."

"And the ants, billions and billions of them, countless generations, you think they're part of a scheme of things? That they serve some inscrutable purpose?"

"It's just that our puny little minds can't see far enough to understand. You admit there's an Intelligence – a Maker of Miracles – so of course there's a purpose too."

"But as I suggested a minute ago, supposing this Intelligence has left?"

"Walked out, you mean? Departed? Come now, that's rather fanciful, isn't it?"

"And in the face of the inscrutable, what's wrong with being fanciful? Supposing that this Intelligence, instead of being an old Know-It-All Greybeard – Don't-You-Dare-Talk-Back-To-Me, one of those – supposing instead, just supposing, he was a Young Fellow, still learning. With a vision of some sort, a lot of bright ideas – some of them maybe half-baked – but not sure how to bring them off. Well then, wouldn't he experiment?"

"And you're actually suggesting—"

"Let's keep on being fanciful: supposing a long time ago He realized we weren't working out, that something had gone wrong – a mistake in the formula, too much potassium – well, mightn't He have gone off somewhere to try again? Another star perhaps, a few thousand light years away. Just left us to run down, tire out, blow ourselves up? So absorbed in his new plans He forgot to pull the switch, so that the machine keeps on turning out the miracles – the not-quite-up-to-scratch miracles – ants, dogs, chickens, us—"

"But you can't be serious!"

"Remember, earlier this evening you asked me what I used to think about on those long drives?"

"Well, I'm afraid I must say how fortunate that the cars came in, to cut down on your travelling time."

"There are a lot of fanciful things in your *Genesis* too, you know. Just another attempt, in fact – not by any means the first or last – to explain and account for the scheme of things. And in a small way, no doubt a very cockeyed way, that's what mine is too. Both of them examples, perhaps, of what you call the puniness of man's mind in the face of the inscrutable. Mine is just considerably punier."

"I'm not sure how to take you. I suppose you mean it humorously – perhaps playing the ever-popular old game of pulling the preacher's leg – but to me, you know, it's blasphemy. A Supreme Intelligence, what I call God – Perfect and Eternal – even to suggest experiments—"

"And why not a little humour too in the face of the inscrutable? Especially since it's all among ourselves. Not one chance in a million your Perfect and Eternal is taking time to listen to the speculations and natterings of an old country doctor. But even supposing He is, do you think what He hears is likely to upset or offend Him?"

"It certainly wouldn't upset Him."

"In His time He's had so much to listen to. Just think of the prayers. When I was a lad I had to go to church every Sunday, sometimes twice, and I remember a preacher who always prayed half an hour straight. I used to time him, a half-hour right to the minute, so he must have timed himself too. A string of *Dear*

Heavenly Fathers just like a column of those ants. But on the subject of experiments, have you ever heard of Dr. Ehrlich?"

"Should I have?"

"He spent a great many years finding a cure for syphilis – long before penicillin – and when at last he had it, a compound of arsenic, he called it 606. That's right, his 606th try. Well, a chance to use that word fanciful again, I've sometimes wondered, supposing we were to take 606 as our scale, where we would be."

"Close?"

"Well, maybe 8 or 9 – or let's be optimistic, coming along in the 400's. Or maybe much closer, nearly there – 601, 605—"

"But not 606?"

"It's all those wasted ants – the old Scotchman in me, I suppose, the thrifty streak, but somehow I feel that my Young Fellow – more blasphemy – wouldn't be satisfied."

"Of course, Doctor, it's not what you believe at all. As I tried to say just a few minutes ago, nothing gives it the lie like your own forty-five years in Upward. If you were convinced the prospect was so bleak, that we were all just so many discards, doomed, you couldn't have carried on, couldn't have cared."

"Bleak? Well, yes and no. Discards, perhaps – nobody up there even aware of us, much less concerned about our fate, nothing working for us but a few traces of intelligence, maybe a little dust and sweat rubbed off from the original contact. But just supposing in spite of everything we could hang on a while, learn to use the intelligence, spread it round—"

"How youthful you sound, Doctor! Doing it all by ourselves, you mean, no help from up there?"

"No help and no interference either. Strictly on our own – sink or swim in our infested, mud-bottomed little Here and Now. The odds, I suppose, not very good, but still you never know . . . .And for that matter it might even be part of the experiment—"

~

"Benny has just issued a warning that a half-minute speech from me will be as much as he can stand, and as I'm sure he speaks for most of you I'm not putting up an argument. We all know why we're here tonight, we all know Doc, so there's not much left to say anyway. He's been saying it himself for the last forty-five years, saying it in ways we'll remember: service and sympathy, sarcasm and bad temper, a sense of duty and a sense of humour; in vile medicine to get even with us for the things we eat and drink, and in a relentless war on pots.

"Each of us will have his or her particular memories, particular reasons for gratitude, but I think what he has meant to me is fairly typical. He was on hand when I was born, he looked after me when I had mumps and measles and whooping-cough, he vaccinated me a couple of times, one Christmas when I was nine or ten he came rushing over to sew up my scalp – brother Stanley had conked me with the poker for stepping on his new aeroplane. Night and day, for weeks, he was with my father when he died, and a few months ago he was on hand again when my own son was born. I grew up on stories about him, my mother's and my grandmother's – all weathers, all roads, how he always got there. . . .

"I haven't forgotten, Benny, I'm cutting down . . . .

"If I've heard it said once in the last few weeks I've heard it twenty times: it's so unfair, just when he's leaving we build a hospital. But I don't think he holds it against us. He hasn't spent forty-five years in Upward without learning something about small-town economics. In the thirties it was the drought and the depression; in the forties, the war. And he knows. He's always been one of us, sharing our lives and problems; he still is and he always will be. It's his hospital. And I don't mean just because we're calling it *The Hunter Memorial*. We're embarrassed because the plaque with his name hasn't come – we had to send to Regina and as today is his birthday we couldn't wait – but plaques don't matter and memories do. It's his hospital.

There aren't many of us who will ever pass it, ever set foot inside, patient or visitor, without thinking of him, seeing him, and whose memories won't be as alive and warm as mine. . . .

"Doc, we've got a watch with an inscription which reads:

> To Sawbones Hunter
> with gratitude and affection
> from Upward
> April 1948
> Many Happy Returns

"We know you have a watch, but this one not only tells the time, it also shows the date and the day of the week, you can read it in the dark, you can keep it on when you're having a bath and you never need to wind it. That's supposed to impress you. In any case we hope you'll wear it and that from time to time it will remind you to drop us a line – or better still, come back for a visit to look us all over and check on our pots again. Just as the watch says, *Many Happy Returns.*"

"It's not a bad-looking watch, Dunc, but if you were timing yourself with it and got all that guff in in half a minute, then the first thing I'll have to do is get it regulated. Just the same, Benny, you've got the right idea: I'm going to cut mine short too. . . .

"Yes, I'll wear it all right. I'll show it off. And don't worry, I'll remember Upward. And one of the things I'll remember – since I'm an old man and know many of you better than you know yourselves, I'll be blunt – one of the things I'll remember, and will probably be puzzling over as long as I'm able to puzzle, is the damfool way you keep spoiling life for yourselves, bringing out the worst in one another. There's so much good here, and you keep throwing it away . . . .

"A family doctor sees a lot of what's going on behind the scenes, and one of the things that has always impressed me is the enormous amount of sympathy and goodwill that springs up the moment someone is in trouble. When there's illness or death, the neighbours rush to help. No second thoughts – one question only: what can we do? They look after the children, bring food, wash clothes, sit up at night. I've often seen so much food coming into a house that the family has had to try giving some of it away again before it spoiled. But then the trouble passes, the household gets reorganized, and this little burst of spontaneous kindness, instead of helping to establish new relationships, make the town an easier, happier place to live in, sputters out in the old bitterness and spite. I'm not taking it on myself to lecture you. Your lives are yours, it's all behind me now, but I can't help saying what a pity, what a waste . . . .

"Just another half minute, Benny, I want to say a few words about the new man. All the reports are good. He'll do a far better job than I've been doing. What I would like to point out, however, is that he can't do it alone. Even with the new hospital – equipment only helps. Many of you remember him, went to school with him, and now that he's coming back to be your doctor you may feel a bit shy, strange. Just remember you probably won't feel half as shy as he will. You went to school with him; he went to school with you. There'll be memories on his side too. And he's going to need all the sympathy and friendliness and trust you can give him. It's only you who can make him feel he belongs here, that he's come to the right place . . . .

"When something goes wrong, when your liver or kidneys or glands start cutting up, it can make a difference how you get along with your doctor. If you like and trust him, things go better. I won't say your trust is half the battle, but sometimes it goes a long way. On the other hand, if you're a hostile patient, suspicious, critical, he'll withdraw a little, give less than he might, no matter how professional or conscientious his care. After all, he's human too. Give him a cold shoulder and he'll give you one back. I say this because I know that not everyone in Upward is ready with a Welcome mat. There are some, I hope not many, who've already set themselves against him, made up their minds, who aren't even willing to take a neutral, wait-and-see attitude. It's unfortunate and unfair. He's done nothing to deserve it. I said just now he's going to need you and all the help you can give him, but in the long run you're going to need him a lot more. He'll be your doctor. It's likely that for at least a few years he's the only one you're going to have . . . .

"Another thing, don't expect miracles. All doctors make mistakes; he'll chalk up a few too. But when something goes wrong don't cluck and say I told you so. Don't start a whispering campaign. Instead give him a chance, try working together. I'll be seeing him for a few hours when he arrives and I could tell him a lot of things about the town, about you, but I don't intend to say a word. I'm not going to so much as breathe on the glass. You'll be his town and he'll be your doctor . . . .

"No matter how well you get along, of course, it's hardly likely he'll be with you forty-five years. The world these days moves at too fast a clip. I only hope that when the time comes, whether it's been a short stay or a long one, you'll have seen to it he leaves as grateful as I am tonight. I only hope that he'll look back and say, as I do, 'They were not wasted years.' "

"Hold it, Doc, just as you are. Now another, looking at the watch this time, just right—"

"Dunc, you and Doc together . . . . And your mother. Come on, Sarah, Dunc's President of the Board and you're President of the Auxiliary – all three of you."

"Oh no, I'm such a sight. I didn't get my hair done—"

"A couple of these geraniums – in the picture they'll look just like a corsage."

"In the centre, Sarah . . . . Oh good Lord, here, take my handkerchief—"

"What about Harry? Harry Hubbs, over here."

"Oh no you don't. You're not getting me to stand up there and make a fool of myself."

"Come on, you're one of his oldest friends. Think of all the money you've taken off him playing poker."

"Now, Mr. Grimble – you and Mrs. Grimble together—"

"Yes, Mr. Grimble. We wanted you to say a prayer but it just didn't seem to work out. Yes, you too, Mrs. Grimble. You and Doc shake hands."

"Doc, over here by the piano. We're mentioning you donated it. And you, Benny, sit down as if you were playing, but be looking at each other."

"What about the Redwing Trio?"

"That's right – Redwing Trio, where are you? Mrs. Billy, Mrs. Jack, Stan – by the piano. And Mrs. Jack, can't you squeeze a little closer to Mrs. Billy so we can get Benny in too?"

"And smile, Mrs. Jack. For Heaven's sake smile. Haven't you heard the good news? *The Lost Chord*'s just been found, a little thin and dehydrated but spirits remarkably high."

"No no, not like that. *Look* at each other, as if you were about to sing *Blest be the tie that binds our hearts in Christian love.*"

"That gives me my caption – *Blest Be the Tie.*"

"Dan Furby, if you dare—"

"Now how about everybody, four deep along the wall – everybody, plenty of room—"

"Good-bye, Doc, good-bye. It was a lovely little speech—"

"Take things easy now and enjoy yourself. You've earned a good rest."

"Don't forget you'll always be welcome. Just drop us a line."

"Good-bye for now. We'll all be down to the train—"

"Dunc wasn't bad – nice and short and not too mushy."

"Caroline, I suppose – or Dan."

"Good-bye and God bless you, Doc. I'll never forget—"

"I wonder who he was hitting at – the Harps?"

"Good-bye, Doc. I just want you to know that I for one will be ready with the Welcome mat."

137

"I still think you ought to be ashamed, walking out at seventy-five."

"Good-bye, Doc, good-bye. Upward's never going to be the same—"

"Well, if ever a man deserved a good drink it's you. Come on home with us for a few minutes, we've got some Scotch . . . . I just want to see everything's all right in the basement and turn out the lights."

"Thanks, Dunc, but Caroline's asked me for dinner tomorrow. I'll wait and have it then."

"A short one. You'll sleep all the better."

"No, it's a nice spring night, I think I'll walk."

"It's freezing again – slippery sidewalks—"

"I've got my rubbers. I'll just take my time."

"Of course, Duncan – he knows the way. And it is a lovely spring night. A little chilly but you can smell April just the same. And a full moon—"

"You're sure? That was a long hard session."

"Feel fine, just want to get the kinks out of my legs."

"Tomorrow then – as early as you like but at the very latest seven. Roast beef, rare, the way you like it—"

"You vant?" and I, not understanding, said "Want what, Anna?"

"You vant?" – a little movement of the hand this time, and all at once a rush a blaze I too.

Knowing without knowing, months and months without knowing, at least a year. Big rough and peasant raw, something like that I would have said. A hunky – look at the handkerchief and feet. All that I saw, that I thought I saw.

Like a horse, a Doukhobor, you could have hitched her up and plowed. Even through her skirt the pump-pump power. Head up and striding – out of my way! Blue eyes – what do you call them, Slavic eyes? no, that's the cheekbones, high and flat – very strong eyes, hard, white-blue, looking you over like a bird. Nick had them too, she passed them on. Eyes and cheekbones both, she saw to it. Wise and careful Anna, not taking chances, thinking ahead so as to give nothing away.

Supposing that is there was anything to give away. Thin little man and always tired, the lungs, the cough, but sometimes they're the kind. Muscles and build and hair on your chest no index to fertility.

"You vant?"

Taking me in too, not just the two bedrooms but the two lives, watching it all with the pale straight eyes, the shrewd-quick peasant pull-a-plow eyes. Husband who is not a husband not a real one – something to be straightened and set right as something in the kitchen she would set right, wipe up spilled milk, put back a plate or close a drawer. Perhaps just that, just seeing things, a job to do—

"You vant?"

Or what I had done for John, poor skinny hollow-chested frightened little John, the bills I never sent, the chickens and eggs – favour for favour, neighbourly return, sleeping alone why wouldn't I want and she, so easy, with so much why shouldn't she?

Nobody's fool at that though – Wednesday afternoon and Ladies' Aid Day, Edith the Good away doing good, Wednesday afternoon in January twenty below and a wind – not many belly-aches that couldn't wait till morning. Did she think of that? Did she think at all? Or was it just a little bump of her hip to close the drawer, just putting the plate away?

"Vas goot . . . "

Question or satisfaction though no way to tell, face with the animation of a snowdrift or a pan of dough. Just like them all when it's over busy with buttons and things, little pats to the handkerchief, a twitch to the hips, but at least no snivelling. Nobody taking advantage of her, oh dear what would my husband say, not like that two-faced Billy bag. Advantage my foot, as if I'd held a gun to her head and her teeth fairly chattering for it – well she wasn't the only one to learn what she could do with her favours, plenty of times back sniffing round for more but oh no my good woman, price above rubies, two in the morning with a glass of water and another two at bedtime, very professional. . . .

No indeed, not Anna, far from snivelling not even a grunt to let me know – there were times I could have wrung her goddam Doukhobor neck although give her her due she maybe didn't know herself. At least not for sure – maybe John all the time was getting a little rock and heave in too. There'd been a girl the first or second year that died, I wormed that much out of her, so at least he knew his way around, what everything was for.

Not a word even when it was time – barely half a day in bed, missed coming only twice and Edith was so pleased, she could let the work pile up. That's one thing about them, just like a cow having her calf; in their own country used to working in the field I suppose – but just the same no more Wednesday afternoons, afraid perhaps there might be another and trouble enough with one.

Cardboard box beside the kitchen stove with a bit of blanket as if he was a litter of pups, and down to the basement with him at the first squawk. No no Anna, you mustn't take him down there. The air's not good, sometimes there's gas from the furnace, remember now – but not a word just the snow-dough face and the snow-dough grunt, waiting till my back was turned. When you come to clean and wash and have to bring the baby you don't let him bother the people you're cleaning for – oh yes, she'd learned a thing or two.

Here, Anna, a little extra this week, there must be things you need, shushing and whispering, conspiracy, Edith upstairs, but again not a word, the bill just stuffed away somewhere and I as excluded as before. Week after week hanging round the kitchen like a little boy waiting his chance to steal a piece of pie, and never so much as a glance or the slightest pressure of her fingers as they closed around the bill. Strictly up to me, if I wanted to, she wasn't asking.

Later the visits, very casual always at supper-time visits – well John and how's the cough these days? sleeping I hope with your window open, remember now right up to the top not just an inch or two. Strange things on the table and stove sometimes, a lot of thick sour milk and thick dark stews – good bone and brain food just the same, better than cornflakes and cake, and whose stomach anyway was going to cope with it? Ah-ha, my Cossack boy, just wait – you'll have your horse, you'll ride the steppes one day!

Nothing for me though in the meantime absolutely nothing all those years but keep on like a butcher boy delivering chickens and eggs. Money no use and no right to interfere, the money just stashed away, bosom to mattress, maybe a hole in the wall. Stubborn peasant thrift tamped tight with alien fear, strange land and stranger tongue, no one to trust or turn to, no way to get the hang of things, people like Edith to crack the whip and watch she didn't waste the soap – nothing to count on but the little wad of bills against the day—

Later still the boots, eight or nine years later, now listen Anna for the last time those aren't the kind, yes I know they're strong but the other boys make fun of them, I want you to go to the store or better let him go himself, and the ten dollars stuffed away with the same little snow-dough grunt and a week later Nick still wearing the old big heavy ones. Time to assert myself, let her see who was running things – now no more nonsense Anna you're supposed to get him shoes, they're spoiling his life it's the other boys, and this time shifty-eyed a second, wavering then sharp, no need new shoes good shoes he got, herself as a child likely barefoot nine months out of twelve. Look Anna, to the store, today, good shoes remember and bring the bill to me. Then I'll pay you and double it – eight on the bill that'll be sixteen for you – that's right I'll double it you understand? oh yes she understood all right, then same little song and dance about the cap, never mind Anna we know it's a warm cap but it's not the kind – this time though quicker, foxy, starting to get wise, you vant again I bring the bill?

The money to him and straight off he'd have taken it to her, and go to the store with him myself it would have been all over town in half an hour – what's Doc taking such an interest in the hunkies for? More shoes, a mackinaw, a suit – always you vant the bill for this one too? vhy not I send to Eaton's, cheaper and you give me just the same – but that was all, never the poor mouth kind, no scheming little hints or sighs. No, not Anna, strictly up to me – just didn't know what she had me by.

Did John suspect? or care? Were there scenes and rows when she bought the cap and shoes? One hand she could have picked him up and hung him on a hook but they say that's the way they are, the man's the one, with all the authority. Just as it should be too, a woman never dares.

Such a scared little man – when it was time for the sanitarium trying to talk him round the way he would take my hand and stare, thinking of what lay ahead for all of them. Just once a little smile, just once that I remember – don't worry about Nick, a fine bright boy I'll keep an eye on him till you're home again, and his face relieved as if far from suspecting, he was close to him and proud, and for all I know was right at that.

Fine boy bright boy and how Daddy used to watch, pretending not to watch. The teacher Shirley something – runaway bowels and white eyebrows – Shirley Shirley doesn't matter, come back in a week I'd say and if there's no improvement we'll try something blander – colitis, yes and no, these cases sometimes very stubborn and how she loved it, all over town what a wonderful doctor I was and such an intellectual too, so interested in new ideas in education. Talk talk the time I wasted just to bring her round to him, the language problems of the New Canadians – haven't you got a Ukrainian boy oh yes indeed we have and coming along just splendidly, as if Daddy didn't know but good fishing anyway. A simply marvellous memory, having to survive in two languages no doubt develops some potential that would otherwise lie dormant – my my my and didn't she know the lovely words! Shirley Shirley . . . wouldn't have taken much persuasion but a little on the fat and rumbly side and I didn't like the eyebrows—

Even poor Dunc, drawing him in too. Want to come along and

watch, why not? some day you never know – and then a couple of months later, just an afterthought, plenty of room in the back seat why not take the hunky too?

The hunky first and the hunky only, shrewd little lewd little minds they'd have lost no time and of course been right at that – listen to the dirty old man complain – and he had a big enough load as it was, Doc Hunter's bastard might have been the straw. A mean trick though on Dunc, I suppose you'd have to say just a little underhand. Such a good boy, steady, willing, making him think perhaps he too – breeding ambitions and desires with who knows how much hurt to follow, maybe a feeling of failure and defeat – the big strong silent kind, you never know—

Although my God he seems adjusted, satisfied. Hospital School and Church Boards, Upward's Citizen Number One, Upward in fact his element. No, he's all right – it's Caroline, what's ahead of her? Right now he's still her handsome hero, humping her nightly as I suppose every woman dreams of being humped you can see it in her eyes, the way she walks, but two or three years when the hump starts levelling off and it's just the groceries and the Boards – oh yes, and coach for the Junior Hockey Team, my God what a man is right.

Both of them though on Nick's side, ready to throw their weight, and the Gillespie weight in Upward should be enough and over. Not in the long run that it matters – wherever he wants to go, he's got the head and hands – but better to stay a while to work it through. Always the sour bit, some of my good friends Ernie Harp and Stan Gillespie, stronger than he is even after eighteen years, every letter gnawing away, and what he is and what they are he shouldn't so much as remember they ever lived. And he knows – must know – Upward of all places, why he said yes, wise enough to understand that sometimes it takes more than buying a ticket and getting on a train . . . Four or five years, just long enough to lay the ghosts, see them for what they are, at times perhaps even pity them, and then, all the little pricks and stings forgotten, healed . . .

So relax, Old Man, go home and sleep. It's all over and it's all beginning, there's nothing more required of you. April and the smell of April, just as it was all beginning that day too . . .

143

You've got your watch and made your little speech, now in you go and up to bed with you. Don't stand in the moonlight doddering at the gate, you're seventy-five you'll catch your death of cold . . . Ugly old barn – we had queer ideas of elegance. Those two little towers, just the place for a nest of owls or witches. And all the gingerbread, the row of little spikes and balls like tassels upside down – before I go we ought to have a shooting match.

The light the light, turn on the light you damned old fool—go stumbling round in the dark you'll fall and break a leg. Old bones are brittle remember, they snap and what kind of exit will that be, down to the train on crutches or in a chair? There . . . just the old bare floors and a couple of crates, you've often seen it worse. What were you afraid of, think one of the owls was going to fly away with you? . . . Used to be matches instead of a switch and sometimes what a hunt and fumble—everything else though just about the same.